Saoirse
the Grey Seal

by
Don Conroy

MENTOR PRESS

This Edition first published 1997 by

MENTOR PRESS
43 Furze Road,
Sandyford Industrial Estate,
Dublin 18.
Tel. (01) 295 2112/3   Fax. (01) 295 2114

ISBN: 0 947548 96 3

A catalogue record for this book is available from the British Library

Cover Illustration: Don Conroy
Editing, Design and Layout by Mentor Press

Printed in Ireland by ColourBooks Ltd.

1 3 5 7 9 10 8 6 4 2

Fill our hearts with tolerance,
Appreciation, and respect
For all living things
So that we all might live together
In harmony and in peace.

Bear Heart

Special thanks to:

Gay Conroy; Brendan, Mary, Orla, Cormac Price (Irish Seal Sanctuary); Dermod Lynskey, Gabriel King; Danny and Kevin McCarthy, the Staff at Mentor Press; Terry, Peter, Stephen Flanagan; Chris Wilson, Líle Ní Chonchúir, John Brennan, Alec Finn, Eithne, Éidín Griffen, Leo Hallissey (CEEC); children of Letterfrack N.S., children of Garristown N.S.; Sylvie Roualt-Allen, ENFO Staff, Tom Collins, Philip Smith, Fingal Sea Food, people of Skerries, Pat Corrigan, Johnnie Woodlock; Trevor Sargent TD, Brendan Howlin TD; Derek Mooney (RTE), Dick Warner (RTE), Ray, Dustin and Socky; Sean Dublin Bay Loftus, Virginia Ferrow, James, Sheila, Flynn, Keith, Trish and John Bowler; Olwyn Fouve, Iarnród Éireann, Garda Síochána, Dave Wall, Damien Nolan; Alan and Kerry of South East Radio, Co. Wexford; King and Subjects of Tory Island, Kevin, Bríd and family, and all of the team at The Winning Post, Co. Wexford.

The Author

Don Conroy is one of Ireland's most popular writers. He has written many books for children and young adults.

Well-known as an artist, wildlife expert and television personality, Don is actively involved in conservation and environmental work.

Contents

Dedicated

to

Gay

with love

Chapter 1

The moonlight shines across the dark waters making a silvery pathway to the island. The waters lap gently on the rocky shore. Under the cover of darkness manx shearwaters and storm petrels head for the land, safe from attack by predatory gulls. Dark green shore crabs patrol the intertidal zone in search of molluscs or dead creatures.

In a small rock pool a blenny surfaces to gulp air. Below the tideline a common starfish moves along the rock, the light-sensitive tips to its arms telling that night has arrived. Limpets begin to forage along the rocks, leaving their snug spots where they clamp on the rocks during the daylight hours. Alongside the limpets the periwinkles feel their way along the bumps and crevices of the rock surface to begin their nightly grazing. An oystercatcher calls as it alights on a nearby rock.

Mara, the grey seal, looks at the celestial canopy. The eternal stars twinkle back. She can hear the heavy breathing of the other seals in the rookery as they sleep soundly. Young pups yelp and suckle in their sleep. Her own son, Saoirse, lies close to her with his head tucked below her foreflipper. Two weeks earlier he was born in a quiet cave on the island where she herself had been born – it was a pupping place for most of the clan.

Her mate, Krail, lies snoring loudly beside her. Mara tries to adjust her position between the sharp rocks. Saoirse snuggles closer. He wants to return to the great heat beyond the damp fur. Licking him affectionately, she lies staring and listening.

Sleep will not come to her since her dream two nights ago, in which she saw the sea boil red with blood. From the sky it rained seals. She recognised them all from the rookery. They sank into the red waters and did not come out again. She called to her newly born pup 'Saoirse! Saoirse!' but he began to vanish from her sight. Then she awoke.

When she told Krail he laughed it off, saying she was anxious because of having given birth recently. Her sister agreed, saying it was because females are channels of life and therefore had a heightened awareness of death as well. Her brother said she was just like their mother, always reading signs and portents into things.

Mara scolded herself and tried to think pleasant thoughts. Hadn't she a good mate who always stood by her, a supportive family which was always there for her, and a beautiful new son who had helped her discover a special kind of love, totally different from her love for Krail, or her family.

As Krail turned in his sleep his whiskered face tickled her shoulder and he laid his foreflipper across her. She settled back and tried to sleep. Then the wind began to pick up. She thought she heard a voice whispering to her on the wind. It seemed to call her name 'Mara! Mara! Beware! Beware!'

Heavy black clouds began to smudge the night sky. Mara became anxious again, she began to see faces in the clouds, angry faces of nusham. There was a loud clap of thunder. Was there death in the thunder? Saoirse trembled in his sleep and inched his head across her body. His sharp teeth were painful to her as he began to suckle. Mara closed her moist brown eyes.

* * *

Matt Keane sat by the hearth in Malachy Ryan's Pub, watching the flames lick up the chimney, his face burnished red from the glow, while flickering shadows danced in the corner of the room.

'More rain,' said Malachy as he listened to it drum on the window pane.

'Feels like winter,' said John Joe, who was standing at the bar. 'I don't know what's happening to the weather these days.'

'Rain, rain, and more rain,' sighed Malachy.

'Pity we couldn't send some to Africa. That's where they need it, with all those droughts,' John Joe added.

'Glad of this fire,' said Matt, sipping his glass of Guinness.

The three musicians sitting in the corner took out their instruments.

'Good on ye,' said John Joe as he watched the fiddle player tune his instrument. The bodhran player warmed up the goat-skin with his big strong hands. The third musician took out a tin whistle and put it to his lips.

'Give us *The Old Women of Ireland*,' said Malachy as he pulled another pint.

The musicians began to play.

'God, it's a lovely air,' said John Joe.

Matt raised his glass approvingly. Suddenly the door swung open and four young men walked in.

'Close that door quickly,' Malachy bellowed. 'That wind will drive out all the heat!'

Matt sat up and watched his son, Michael, enter carrying a heavy hessian sack. 'Good night to you all,' said Malachy. 'What will I get you?'

'The usual,' said Michael gruffly, placing the sack upright against the wall. His three friends, Francis, Gerry and Peadar moved towards the heat of the fire.

'What's in the sack?' Matt inquired.

Michael hadn't noticed his father sitting in the corner of the pub. He stared hard at him. 'Oul hawk-eye spots everything,' said Michael taking his pint from the counter.

'Well, it's not fishing gear,' Gerry sniggered.

'Son, I asked you what's in the sack.'

'I'm bloody twenty-six years old and he still treats me like a little school boy.' Michael put the pint on a shelf and opened the string around the sack. The sack fell loose, revealing three rifles and a shotgun. Michael picked up the .22 rifle and ran his hand along the barrel.

The music stopped. There was an uneasy silence.

'Don't worry,' said Peadar, breaking the silence. 'We're not going to rob you,' he added, looking at Malachy.

'I wouldn't wonder at anything these days,' Malachy retorted.

Gerry picked up the shotgun and looked down the barrel.

'Put those damn things away,' Matt ordered his son. 'And tell me why you have them.'

'Well, it isn't to shoot grey crows,' claimed Gerry.

Matt stared hard at his son. 'Well?'

'We're off to the island tomorrow to sort out those damned water rats.'

'What water rats?' asked Malachy.

'You want to kill the seals, is that it?' Matt demanded.

'Yes, those bloody grey seals,' Michael hollered. 'I'm sick of them eating my fish, and destroying the nets.'

'I can understand your frustration, son,' said his father warmly. 'But the seals have to live as well.'

'They were here before us,' Malachy added. 'And they'll be here long after us.'

'Not this lot,' said Peadar. 'We will get them tomorrow, that's a promise.'

'I've lived most of my life on the water, son, as you well know. We've lived alongside the seals and the rest of God's creatures and always managed to feed a family. The sea will provide for all, son, if you treat her well.'

'Well said, Matt,' added John Joe. 'Nowadays people use the sea like a washing machine, throwing in all kinds of rubbish, polluting the very thing that gives them their livelihood.'

'And what about all the fish that are dumped because they don't get the market price?' asked Malachy. 'A terrible waste of nature's bounty.'

'I know what's happening,' snapped Michael. 'I don't need a lecture on ecology. The fact remains that the colony has become too large and they're emptying the waters around here.'

'Well, that's not the way things work,' said one of the young musicians. 'The seal numbers, like all predators, depend on their prey. If there is plenty of food there will be an increase in predators, if there's a shortage of food the predators numbers drop drastically.'

'They're all watching too many National Geographic programmes on that!' claimed Gerry, pointing at the television with the shotgun.

'Well, let me tell you all I didn't come in here to debate the merits of ecology. This is a local problem and it's going to be dealt with at local level by the four of us.' Michael finished his pint, picked up the sack and the guns. 'Let's get out of here. See you Sunday,' he grunted at his father, and left with the others, slamming the door behind him.

'What's got them so worked up?' Malachy wondered.

Matt threw another log on the fire. 'I think himself and Bridie are not hitting it off too well.'

'That's a pity,' said John Joe. 'Ah sure, they're still adjusting to married life. It's hardly two years since they tied the knot.'

'I'm still adjusting,' said Malachy, 'and I'm married thirty five years.' They laughed loudly. 'Here, you can all have a glass on me. The night that's in it and all.' Then looking at the musicians: 'Hey are you lot in the corner going to give us a few more songs or sit there as part of the furniture?' The musicians laughed and began to play.

Chapter 2

Like a shroud, a heavy fog hung over the island and spilled out to sea. Visibility was poor. Mara had managed to get some sleep and was not troubled by any nightmares. The rookery was stirring; there was a cacophony of noise. Saoirse was still sleeping. Krail was very alert, watching the young males who were in the water, heads bobbing and hoping for a chance to mate as soon as the pups were weaned.

Krail pulled himself into an upright position, displaying his power and strength. He growled several times, warning any would-be suitors to keep well away from his ten wives. Other males did the same, showing their strength and determination to protect their harems.

A fulmar flew by on stiff wings above Mara. Then she thought she heard a low constant noise from the sea. It was difficult to concentrate above the noise. She nudged Krail to listen, explaining that she had heard a noise. Krail became attentive and listened hard, but neither he nor Mara could hear anything unusual. She began to relax again.

Saoirse was awake, staring up at her with his big brown moist eyes. 'Hungry again?' she asked gently, and heeled over on her side. Saoirse bleated, and nuzzled her.

Mara stared hard out to sea. In the enveloping fog something began to take form. A boat came into focus. There was the sound of voices, nusham whispering.

Krail growled. He could see clearly the shape of the small boat with four men on board. They had cut the engine and were drifting closer to the island. Fear spread through the rookery. The seals were all now fully awake and alert. Those in the water began to haul themselves out on to the land away from the vessel.

Mara barked loudly and tried to conceal Saoirse below her body. Saoirse pulled away. He wanted to see this strange object floating in the water. Krail boomed the alarm call. He had seen many a vessel fishing off-shore but he knew there was something different about this one.

Mara could see the nusham faces. They were the same angry faces she had seen in the storm clouds. The pups, sensing the tension, began to climb on to their mothers, making a whimpering noise.

'They're like sitting ducks,' yelled Peadar as he pointed the rifle.

'Make sure none of them escapes,' hollered Michael Keane.

The four men took aim with their rifles and shotgun.

The seals clustered together. There was a deathly silence. They sat, transfixed with terror. The silence was quickly shattered by loud gunfire. Fire and smoke belched from the barrels.

Saoirse's fascination was suddenly interrupted by the explosion of noise.

A searing pain shot through Mara's body. She was the first to be hit. She twisted and collapsed. A terrible panic ran through the rookery. Seals crashed into each other as they tried to climb over the sharp rocks for shelter. Pups were accidentally trampled in the panic that ensued. Krail moved hurriedly to Mara. He was hit on the shoulder and began bleeding badly.

Another round of gunfire followed quickly after the first. Krail was hit twice in the head. He crashed down on to a rock, jerked several times, then lay still.

Saoirse watched paralysed with fear as one member of his

family after another was hit by the deadly bullets, their bodies twisting in mid-air, ribs shattering and limbs crushing under the force of the fall. Fur that had been sleek and glossy was now matted with blood. Still the sound of gunfire rang out.

'To hell with you all,' Michael Keane yelled as he emptied his rifle into another seal.

The great beasts lay dying, each one bleeding and groaning. The dying was hard and long for some of the seals. Two of the men jumped onto the rocks with pick handles and clubbed the wounded and the dying.

'I think we've got them all,' yelled Francis.

'That's what you call a proper cull,' said Gerry, gripping the blood-stained handle and laughing nervously.

'Right,' said Michael, as he stared at the blood-red water. 'Let's get out of here.'

They turned on the engine and sped away.

An eerie silence descended on the island.

*   *   *

Saoirse, huddled under his mother's fallen form, began to wriggle himself free. His senses were reeling from everything he had seen. His eyes stared wide at the carnage. Frozen forms of seals lay strewn about. There was red oozing from wounds where the bullets had penetrated fur and flesh.

Saoirse sat heavy with grief among the slumped figures. His stomach churned and heaved at the terrible sight of severed limbs and smashed skulls. He wailed for his mother and nuzzled her hard, nestling up to the wounded body. He heard his name being whispered.

'Saoirse!' Air tore out of her lungs as she gasped and spoke in a choking voice. 'Thank the great spirit you are alive, my child.' There was warmth in her moist eyes. Saoirse nudged her

to get up. 'Listen my son,' she said weakly. 'You must live; the sea will be your mother now. I am going to rest on a different shore. You cannot come with me, but we shall meet again when the great ocean of time will bring you back to us again.' With great effort she moved her foreflipper and laid it across him. Then she spoke slowly and sadly. 'The death guns have robbed you of family and security, but they have not robbed you of the gift of life. It is a very special thing but it must not be squandered; it is to be lived to the full. I make this last wish for you that you find friendship and joy in life. You are of noble birth. You must carry on our great colony and not let it end here like this.'

Saoirse only wanted to be with Mara and his father. She gave a deep sigh and a heave. Her mouth hung open, warm blood trickled out, dampening his creamy fur. Saoirse watched as her life ebbed away. He felt a terrible emptiness inside. Mara's body which had radiated heat, so much heat it was fire itself, was now cold to the touch. Try as he might, Saoirse could not get the smell of blood from his nostrils. It hung in the air like a noxious vapour. He lay silent and still for a long time.

The chilly wind began to pick up and whipped around him numbing his face. Something within began to spur him on. He ignored it for as long as he could, until finally he began to rouse himself. He pulled himself past the silent remains of his dead family and friends. Then he edged himself out onto the ledge of a large rock. He nosed the wind and stared at the pearl grey sky. He hissed and spat in anger.

What debt did his family owe to destiny that they must pay in full with blood? He was not answered. He stared at the icy water in lonely silence. He thought he heard a voice on the wind, very faintly running between the waves. It began to clarify. It was a female voice calling to him: 'Saoirse, Saoirse'.

The waves seemed to reach out, beckoning him. Then the voice sounded in his head again. 'Come, unlock the secrets of the sea, come, don't be afraid.' Saoirse edged closer to the sea.

Suddenly screams jolted him back onto the rock. Overhead hundreds of gulls were wheeling around the sky like dark clouds, swooping low and calling in a demonic chatter. Great black-backed gulls and those pirates of the sea, the skuas, all circled like vultures over the island. They had seen from a distance what had happened. Now that it was safe they came to feed on the remains.

The screams of the gulls frightened Saoirse. A great black-backed gull landed on his back and began to pull at his fluffy white fur. Saoirse barked and snapped, then scurried into a nearby rock pool, almost completely submerging himself. The gulls were making a dreadful clamour as they picked at the dead bodies, tearing large chunks of flesh from them, their strong bills picking at the holes made by the bullets and getting to the tender parts beyond the fur and blubber.

More gulls arrived, harrying the first lot from their positions. Fights broke out between them. Immature gulls stood on the sidelines waiting to pinch a morsel from the adults. The frenzied feeding continued for most of the day. Gulls sat around heavy with food from all the gorging.

Saoirse watched from the safety of the rock pool.

The gulls reduced the rookery to nothing more than skulls and bones. Even the crabs had come from their hiding places to feed on this unexpected bounty. In the rock pool, unknown to Saoirse, life and death struggles were unfolding. A sea anemone, firmly attached to the rocks, had unfolded its tentacles. A common shrimp passed by, not realising the danger in these tentacles. Tiny stinging harpoons shot out from them attacking the shrimp and piercing its skin with their backward pointed barbs – these inject the victim with a lethal venom which destroys its nervous system. The shrimp broke into violent convulsions, then succumbed to death.

The anemone was not to enjoy its meal, for another beaded anemone attacked it. They fought for several moments stinging each other until the first anemone loosened itself from the rock and retreated away to a different spot, while the beaded anemone fed on the dead shrimp.

It was almost nightfall before the gulls finally departed from the island to roost on another island. They drifted away silently like dark spectres across the crimson sky, leaving the island to Saoirse and the dead.

*   *   *

Saoirse hauled himself out of the pool. The evening was cold. He sniffed the air and hoped the rising wind would dry him quickly. He stared at the star-studded sky and then lay down, covering his face with his foreflippers. His mind was so confused that the nightmarish visions began to flood back across his brain.

As the night wore on he became more terrified. It was the first time he had ever been alone. There was no warm body to snuggle up to, no warm face staring back at him, no friends to play games with. Only the rocks and the sea.

He was hungry and his body ached. He began to weep again. The grief was like an intense pain in his head, completely overwhelming his senses. He wept until he could weep no more. Then he saw something move in the silvery tipped waves. He knew the shape; it was his mother. She was moving to the rhythm of the waves.

He raised his head and hurried to the edge, whimpering. Haunting voices called again on the wind. Ghostly forms and spirits shimmered through the white foam. It was his family and friends calling to him. They joined with his mother in the waves, playing their games and porpoising in the water.

Saoirse so wanted to join them. But as he watched with astonishment the water swallowed them. Yet he could still hear Mara speaking to him. Her voice was so sweet, her words strange. We are now immortals my son, we have gone from the world of substance. Gather your courage and follow your destiny. Saoirse watched the magical light dancing on the waves, then her voice whispered again. Remember, the sea is now your mother. She calls you, you must heed her call. Then the visions were gone.

Saoirse scanned the waters but could not see her. He called and called.

The gentle whispering waves in their steady rhythm began to make him feel calm and relaxed. Soon he was lulled to sleep.

Chapter 3

Saoirse roused himself and blinked in the bright morning light. He scratched himself with his long slender claws, then stretched his paddle-shaped foreflippers and began to pull himself over the slippery rocks towards the water. His whiskery face twitched as he nosed the water. It was cold.

A kittiwake sailed by overhead; in the distance a cormorant could be seen diving for food. Saoirse was impressed when he saw it surface with a fish in its bill. He barked in a begging way at the bird. It ignored his pleas, swallowed the fish and continued to dive. The sight of the fish made Saoirse very hungry. It was time he entered the water.

His mother had said he should be catching fish for himself by the next full moon, which was only a few days away. He looked over his shoulder at the bones of his relations, at the empty sockets of the skulls, and knew that if he just lay about he would soon starve. He stared back to sea. A puffin sped low over the waves. Saoirse wondered what life would be like under the waves.

He was still very apprehensive. If only Mara or Krail were here to coax him in it would be so easy; he wouldn't give it a second thought. But they were gone, and he was at the edge of life's great adventure. All he had to do was slip into the water. He was a sea creature like all his kin. There was his real home, a wave away. The water lapped gently below.

Go, get in, he ordered himself. Are you afraid? he scolded himself. If a bird can do it, surely he could. He scanned the waters. They were calm, no boats or nusham, just the water and a few sea birds. He tensed his body. He would do it now; he must! On an impulse he pushed his body forward over the rocks, then plop! And he was in the water.

He shivered from the shock of the cold, then began to propel himself forward from the rear, pushing against the water using his foreflippers for steering. Movement seemed so much easier than on land, where it was more laboured. He stuck his face below the water; he could not see the bottom. He felt afraid but strangely exhilarated. The water lapped against his body. It felt good. He waded out further, keeping his head high out of the water. His body began to relax and he became more confident.

Then out of nowhere, it seemed, a great black-backed gull appeared. It circled above his head, then alighted on his back and pecked him on the nape of the neck pulling a chunk of

white fur. Saoirse growled loudly and wriggled his body to free himself from this pest. The gull pecked again only this time on the top of his head. Saoirse let out a squeal of pain. The gull soon tired of this activity and flapped away.

Saoirse was not any the worse for the attack but became panicked and stopped at the water's surface. With his foreflippers he began to turn in circles and started bleating loudly. No one seemed to hear. A wave washed over him, taking him unawares. Water filled his nostrils and his mouth. He coughed and sneezed.

On again out into this mass of water. Strong waves began buffeting him. He became more and more concerned as he struggled under the hostile conditions. He watched the waves rising and falling. They began to reach over him again. This time he was more prepared. He closed off his nostrils and his mouth as each wave covered him.

He began to wonder would he ever settle into life at sea. The going was getting tougher and tougher. He was becoming exhausted and his body ached. The hunger pangs were getting worse. He decided to turn back to the island. Perhaps he could find some food in the rock pool. He needed to rest.

He remembered seeing other seals dozing in the water with only their snouts appearing above the waves. He was afraid to try it. All he wanted to do was haul himself out on a smooth rock, sheltered from the winds, and rest. On he moved through the grey waters unaware that his fur was becoming water-logged. He wondered was he swimming in the right direction for the island seemed to be getting further away from him. He was becoming disorientated. The waves seemed to reach out to him and claw him like some strange beast and he fought against their pull.

Then he felt himself being sucked below the surface. He gasped and felt a choking sensation. He tried to call for help but could not find his voice. He was going down deeper into the bowels of darkness.

He struggled to free himself. It was as if a strange beast had him within its mouth. Like powerful jaws the waves closed over him. He was being swallowed up by the water.

Then a deadly silence enveloped him. Angry faces began to loom large in a swirling vortex. The anger turned to laughter on the nusham faces as they watched him struggle for air. The ocean was now a dark abyss where he was floating to his certain doom. Terrifying shapes began to replace the men's faces from the penetrating darkness. Poisoning spirits wanted to inhabit him. They flashed deadly fangs.

The darkness was now within him. Weird melancholic voices called him to death. Saoirse felt an overwhelming desire to succumb to death. Down, down, he drifted. He began to relax and not struggle, just let things happen to him. Life had cheated him of his family and friends. The great fire of love was quenched. He was now willing to accept death, for all his loved ones had entered through its gates. He was ready to embrace it and become an immortal.

Then he heard Mara's voice in his head. No, my son! No, you must live! Live! Do not come to death this way! It will come to you as a friend some day, not like an enemy. Saoirse, wake up! Saoirse!

A dark shape moved below him.

*　*　*

Saoirse opened his eyes and then began to cough. Water poured from his mouth and nostrils. He retched several times as more water emptied from his stomach. Half-submerged, Saoirse looked at the rock which he was lying across. He didn't know how he'd managed to pull himself onto it, but he was very grateful. His foreflippers held tightly to the sharp ridges for there was water all round, as far as he could see in every direction.

The island was gone. Maybe it too was swallowed by the water. Up ahead shearwaters weaved in and out between the waves. A shag sat on the water, ever alert. Saoirse noticed that the rock was drifting towards it. The shag began to get anxious, then started to take off over the waves. It took a few seconds to become airborne, then flew low over the water and alighted a good distance away.

Saoirse was sure he had passed the exact spot where the shag sat a few minutes earlier. How amazing for he had never known a rock to float before.

'How are you feeling, little fella?' Saoirse pulled himself into alertness and looked around to see who was speaking. But there was no one about. 'You've been through a terrible ordeal for one so young.'

The voice was warm and friendly. Saoirse realised it was

coming from the edge of the rock. He pulled himself to the front and found himself looking into a dark head with two large eyes, one on either side of the face.

'Hope you're getting a bit of a rest back there. The water is quite choppy, so hold on good and tight!' Saoirse had never seen a creature like this before. It seemed friendly but could he trust it.

'What's your name?' asked the leathery turtle.

'A grey seal,' said Saoirse.

'I know you're a grey seal, sure haven't I wandered the great oceans and the seven seas. Do you have a name?'

'Saoirse,' he replied.

'Saoirse, that's a fine name. I'm Lutra. I don't suppose you've seen many like me before?'

'No,' said Saoirse. 'You're certainly strange looking.'

'Thanks!'

'No, I didn't mean it the way it sounded, it's just . . . '

'I understand!' said the bemused turtle. Then his tone darkened. 'I saw what happened to the colony. A terrible massacre.' Then he added: 'The nusham are a strange species indeed. Sometimes they act better than any other creatures I know, other times worse. I've been around nearly a century and I certainly can't fathom them.

Not that I've had much direct contact with them. More a case of observing them down through the years.'

Saoirse said nothing. If he never met another nusham for as long as he lived that would suit him fine. For he had never seen any other creature kill purely for pleasure except those nusham.

On they moved to the rhythms of the sea. Saoirse wondered why this strange turtle would bother to rescue him and show him such kindness. He certainly felt no fear from this creature.

'I have been so terribly afraid since my clan was wiped out,' Saoirse admitted.

The turtle gulped air and said sadly: 'That kind of horror, seeing your own being slaughtered, I don't know whether a pain like that will ever dull with time. One can only hope. But remember . . . ' the turtle added, 'the truly brave are afraid but go on despite their fear. The fear and tragedy we creatures experience must be offered up on the great altar in the wild place.'

Saoirse didn't understand what Lutra meant, but the voice was calm and reassuring. He yawned and lay his head back down on the carapace.

'You rest up little fella, and I'll take you to a place where you will get food and be secure.'

Saoirse yawned a 'thank you'. The gentle whispering waves lulled him to sleep.

*   *   *

Saoirse roused himself. There was an impression of his head in the soft sand. He sneezed and wiped the sand from his nostrils with his foreflipper. Where was he, he wondered. He looked around but nothing was familiar. The rocks and sand were totally different from his island. Still, it felt good to have dry land under him. He wondered where was Lutra, the turtle that had rescued him.

Saoirse stretched his whole body. He was completely rested. All the aches and pains were gone. Then a shadow passed over, completely covering him. Saoirse turned around. A great beast stared at him. Saoirse was completely taken by surprise as he stared at the massive seal.

'How are you feeling?' the voice boomed at him.

'Well, thank you,' Saoirse answered, trembling all over.

The penetrating grey eyes of the male seal seemed to bore through him. 'I expect you're hungry,' said the adult seal gruffly. Saoirse nodded. 'Follow me,' the seal commanded.

Saoirse pulled himself along. Then the male seal stopped. Saoirse crashed into him. 'Oops, sorry,' said Saoirse.

'I better introduce myself. I am Grypus, the oldest seal in Ireland. I was once known as the Prince of the Seas. Most of the colonies along the west coast are related to me. Including you! You haven't told me your name.'

'I'm called Saoirse.'

'Who were your parents?'

'Mara and Krail were their names.'

The old male sighed deep in his heart. 'They will be sorely missed.' Then staring at Saoirse he said warmly: 'You can be

proud of them. Their names will be written in the waves and winds for ever.'

Saoirse stared at the huge grey form of Grypus as he picked up a flounder. 'Here!' He tossed the fish at Saoirse. The pup put his foreflippers on the fish and licked the flesh. He wasn't quite sure how to eat it. Grypus picked up a mackerel and swallowed it down head first. Sensing Saoirse's difficulties he stretched over and took a bite out of the side of the fish. 'There, that should get you started. Take small pieces at a time. Very soon you will be able to swallow fish whole, but for now take it easy until you get the hang of it.'

A watchful herring gull swooped down and snatched the flounder from Saoirse and quickly flew away. Saoirse bleated in pleading tones.

Grypus stared hard at the young pup. 'Stop bleating! Bark and snap at those scavenging gulls, otherwise they'll rob the eye out of your head. Show them who's in command.' Grypus threw him over a mackerel. 'Don't lose that,' he snapped.

Saoirse sheepishly picked at the fish, watching Grypus tear into a large ling.

Grypus looked out to sea. His eyes brightened as Lutra the turtle hauled himself out of the water. 'How's the young fella feeling?' Lutra enquired.

'Hasn't lost his appetite,' said Grypus, speaking for him. There was a calmness in his voice. The three of them lay about on the soft sand. The waves licked at Grypus' hind flippers. Lutra pulled some kelp that was tangled around his left flipper. Saoirse could smell the rotting seaweed on the shoreline, while the living seaweed was wafting gently with the currents beside the rocks.

'How is my dear friend Lutra?' Grypus enquired.

'As well as can be expected. Next year I'll be celebrating my hundredth birthday.'

'You're nearly a century old,' said Saoirse in awe.

'Oh yes,' blinked the old grey eyes. 'Sometimes I feel it in these old bones.'

'Nonsense, you're good for another fifty years,' Grypus grinned.

'Maybe,' said Lutra. 'But it's not getting any easier roaming the ancient seas. What with all the new pollutants that these nusham throw into our homes – a nightmare even to the great whales. And those plastic bags! One of my relations mistook one for a jellyfish, swallowed it and a few weeks later it was dead. As for those things called balloons that nusham send into the sky when they're really happy, later they fall into the sea and dolphins, fish and birds eat them thinking they're some new kind of food. They too end belly up after eating them.'

'And what about the black substance that they let spill out of their tankers?' Grypus added.

'Oh yes, the oil, that's terrible altogether. What I can't

understand is, if the humans like to fish why do they dump all this rubbish into the sea?' Lutra sighed.

'I wish I could dump the stuff on their land,' growled Grypus. 'Maybe if they could see the mess it makes they mightn't be so casual about dumping it in the sea.'

'Sadly, I don't think it would work,' said Lutra. 'A common gull told me once they are just as bad on the land, dumping in beautiful places, poisoning rivers and lakes. Sending deadly smoke into the air.'

'Something should be done,' Grypus bellowed. 'If there was only some way to communicate with them, some way to tell them we all need to share the planet together. No one species can hold the others up to ransom. They're like some kind of virus on the planet destroying all around them.'

'Even the ones that obey them don't get an easy passage. The dogs, horses, cats, cows, sheep and others, they don't get it much better,' said Lutra. 'I've seen enough over these years to make your fur stand on end.'

'Let's change the subject,' said Grypus. 'It only upsets me. Besides, we don't want to put young Saoirse off the great thrill of living in two worlds.'

'Too true,' said Lutra. 'I'm getting a bit cranky in my old age. I must watch that. Do you know, young Saoirse, on distant shores you have many relations?' Saoirse shook his head. 'Some are very small like you, and they're adults!' Saoirse was amazed. 'They're called the ringed seal, and they live in the cold world of the Arctic. And there's the fur seal of the Galapagos, that's pretty small too. Then you have the biggest seal, even bigger than old Grypus here.' Grypus snorted in mock annoyance.

'What's its name?' asked Saoirse.

'The elephant seal,' said Lutra. 'Then there's the walrus with two big tusks of ivory coming out from his upper jaw.'

'Tusks indeed,' said Grypus. 'Maybe it's the walrus that should be called the elephant seal.'

'Good point,' said Lutra, then he added: 'You do know that on occasion they visit these parts?'

'Of course I do,' said Grypus. 'Not much happens around here without my knowing.'

Then Lutra turned to Saoirse. 'There are sea lions, they have little ear lobes sticking out.' In hushed tones he continued, 'The nusham have been known to capture them and put them into zoos, where they must entertain the nusham before they get any food.'

Grypus explained what a zoo was.

'I wouldn't fancy that,' said Saoirse. 'I'd hate to be gawked at all day by nusham.'

'Then there's the leopard seal, the monk seal, the bearded, the harp, the ribbon . . . '

'Maybe, Lutra, we should tell young Saoirse about the food he should be catching around here, and not fill his mind with too many exotic things. He'll only end up with a wanderlust and never settle down to start his own colony.'

Saoirse enjoyed hearing about all those strange relations but did not want to disagree with Grypus. Besides, talking about food was just as fascinating.

'Fish will be essential to your diet, young Saoirse. Salmon is one of my favourites, but I only have it on a special occasion. Don't refuse a meal of squid or shellfish, indeed some of the crustaceans can be quite delicious. Another tasty meal is sand eels, of course you need to eat quite a lot of them.'

Grypus stopped and began to scratch his fur with his

foreflipper. Saoirse began to imitate him. Scratching felt very good indeed. Then to his horror, chunks of white fur came out the harder he scratched,

Grypus noticed the anxiety coming over the young pup. 'Don't alarm yourself, young fella. That's only natural. Soon you'll lose all that white fur and grow a beautiful sleek coat like mine.'

Saoirse looked at the tears, bite marks, and scars on the old seal's fur, but said nothing.

'Well, what I mean is,' said Grypus, aware that his fur was not in great condition, 'you will develop a beautiful adult coat very soon. Your baby fur will soon be gone, and your puppy ways too I hope. In the meantime you are welcome to stay here until you are strong and can fend for yourself. This is the way of the wild folk and you must be ready for the challenge. Now, I must rest. The night is upon us already.'

Grypus pulled himself over to a larger boulder and settled down behind it. 'Good night, Lutra. Good night, Saoirse.'

Lutra pulled himself down to the water. 'I prefer to sleep here.' He yawned and settled in the shallow water.

Saoirse looked at the full moon that was hanging in the sky.

'Lutra, Lutra,' Saoirse called.

'What is it?' said a drowsy turtle.

'Where did the moon come from?'

'The moon!' he exclaimed.

'Yes,' said Saoirse. 'I've seen it before.'

Lutra chuckled quietly. 'Long, long ago, when the earth was young and her oceans were of a liquid fire, she gave birth to her daughter the moon. Then she sent her out into the night sky where she hangs and shines her pale light to help wild folk find their way in the dark. I think you should rest now,' the turtle yawned.

Chapter 4

Saoirse poked his head up and sniffed the crisp air. He noticed an arrowhead of birds passing high over the island. Beyond the sharp fingers of rock a grey heron stood motionless. Head and neck were tucked in giving it a squat appearance. As soon as Saoirse shifted his body the heron stood in alertness and bobbed its head several times. Reaching out its long snake-like neck to view this young seal, it then settled back into a resting position, realising it was in no danger.

Saoirse was amused to see Grypus dozing in the calm waters. He sat vertically in the sea with his nose poked above the surface, his hind flippers pushing him upwards when the water would cover over his nose.

Saoirse decided to brave the water again. He pulled himself down to the edge and gingerly faced into the shallow water. It felt cold but good. He loved the tingling sensation. Chunks of white fur came away from his body and floated on the surface.

'How are you, young fella?' enquired Lutra, who seemed to appear from nowhere.

'Great,' said Saoirse, then added, 'a bit hungry.'

'Well, we'll all need breakfast but first let's sneak up on ol' Grypus. Follow me,' said Lutra as he passed the shallow shelf and dived deep into the dark waters.

Saoirse followed, not giving it a second thought. When he realised he was so far from the surface he became tense.

'Take it nice and easy,' said the turtle, sensing Saoirse's fear. Lutra's voice calmed him, his breathing relaxed and became slower and stronger. They stole across the ocean bed until they were directly below Grypus. Then they sneaked up on the old

seal and nipped him on the hind flippers.

Grypus awoke with a loud growl. 'What the devil is going on? Who dares try to challenge me?' he bellowed with spluttering breath, his battle-scarred body twisting and swirling in annoyance, the water foaming about him.

Saoirse and Lutra bobbed up alongside him. 'Good morning Grandad,' said Saoirse cheerfully.

'Slipping up,' said Lutra. 'If we were able to sneak up on you, imagine a hungry orca would think it was its birthday to catch a big prize like you.'

'Just let it try,' growled Grypus. 'Besides, I always sleep with one eye open. Of course I knew all along it was you two up to mischief. I let you indulge in your little games.'

Lutra winked at Saoirse.

'It was fun,' said Saoirse.

'Well, while you two were snoring your heads off earlier I was out getting breakfast. Someone has to provide for you lazy bones.'

Saoirse felt very happy and began swirling and dancing upon the sea, then diving deep and returning to the surface. Grypus and Lutra watched with joy as Saoirse frolicked in the water.

'He has suffered a lot for one so young,' said Grypus to Lutra. There was a sadness in his voice. Saoirse exploded out of the water and startled a kittiwake that was flying low over the waves. Then he nose-dived back into the swell, tossing about in the waves.

'Time for breakfast,' Grypus bellowed as he paddled back to dry land followed by the leathery turtle. Saoirse hurried to join them. He didn't want to miss out on food. Strewn about was some cod, ling, haddock and several jellyfish for Lutra. Saoirse grew ravenous at the sight of the fish, then he gave out a plaintive cry.

'No need for all that,' said Grypus. 'Just get stuck in.' Saoirse watched Grypus swallow a fish. Saoirse gave a whimper. 'Stop whinging and eat up. Swallow head first.'

Saoirse gripped the smaller fish, threw his head back and began to swallow the fish. He made several choking noises but did manage to swallow the fish whole. Saoirse looked at a rather strange fish which the old seal was about to polish off. 'It's a conger eel, just as tasty as any fish but a bit tricky to catch. You can find them skulking in the old shipwreck on the sea bed.' He continued to gorge himself on the eel. Meanwhile Lutra was chomping down on a jellyfish. 'How can you eat that gunge,' Grypus remarked. 'I prefer a nice meaty fish myself.'

The turtle looked up once. 'They're delicious,' said Lutra, his jaws bubbling with jellyfish.

Grypus swallowed a haddock, then crashed down on the soft sand. He belched. 'Ah, that's better.'

Saoirse crashed down beside him feeling nice and full. Then

he looked at the old seal and said. 'What's an orca?'

Grypus pulled himself into an upright position. 'Don't mention orcas after I've eaten. It's enough to give me indigestion.' Grypus hauled his heavy frame over to the rocks, stopping at a boulder with a sharp cornered edge to it. There he began rubbing his flanks up and down on the edge. Saoirse watched his rippling flesh heaving up and down in wild jerky movements.

Lutra beckoned Saoirse over. 'I'm afraid you've upset him, talking about orcas.' They looked over at Grypus who ignored them, and just continued to scratch deeper and deeper. 'He'll stay scratching there for ages. It's not so much that he has an itch, it's just that having a good scratch relaxes him. Then he'll rest up and hopefully later he will be in better form.'

Saoirse twitched but said nothing. 'You see, young fella, seals have few enemies out there.' He gestured with his head towards the water. 'Of course, the nusham seems to be the enemy of all creatures. Then there are his deadly poisons which he pours into our seas from his work places. These lethal liquids kill many creatures including seals. Some seals will fight each other especially during the mating season. So be careful, young Saoirse, not to upset any young or indeed old bulls when the breeding season comes along.'

'I will,' said Saoirse. 'Don't you worry.'

Then the old turtle stared into the seal's eyes. 'There is another deadly creature which roams the seas in search of seals and fish. This is the orca or killer whale. Seals call it the dark shadow. It is a large powerful whale with a long dorsal fin, and a big mouth full of sharp teeth. It moves through the water at lightning speed. Sometimes you may get a glimpse of its black dorsal fin cutting through the water. But most of the time it

will sneak up from below when seals are dozing or playing just below the surface. Just like the way we did on old Grypus.'

Saoirse swallowed hard and stared out to sea.

Then Lutra said in brighter tones. 'Of course, they are rare around these parts and if one does appear it's usually in a pod in pursuit of a large shoal of fish.'

Saoirse realised then why the mention of an orca sent old Grypus into a flap.

The turtle yawned and stretched then added. 'Fancy a swim?' The young seal looked anxious. 'You're not afraid?'

'No,' said Saoirse nervously. They looked over at Grypus who was sound asleep.

'I'll race you to the water,' said Lutra. Saoirse thrust his head forward and with a quick burst of speed reached the water's edge in seconds. Lutra struggled slowly after him, then slipped into the water. Once in the water the turtle moved with grace and speed past Saoirse and on out into the deep.

It felt so good to be back in the water that Saoirse quickly forgot any fears and began to roll and splash in the calm waters, leisurely porpoising for a time then returning to some rolling and splashing. There was plenty of time to explore the marine world but for now he was content to loaf about with the turtle.

Lutra kept diving deep then returning briefly for a gulp of air. Saoirse would try to guess where he would pop up next. He would chase to a spot where he thought the old turtle would surface and slap the water with his foreflipper hoping to startle Lutra. The turtle was always too clever and kept outwitting him, despite several attempts at a surprise attack.

As Lutra surfaced again a distance away from Saoirse he noticed something surface in the distance. Gulls were wheeling and squabbling overhead. As he tried to identify the object he was suddenly pounced on by the young seal, which winded him, making him swallow a quantity of sea water. He coughed and spluttered as he resurfaced.

'Got you that time,' Saoirse chuckled, as he threw himself on his back and propelled himself away from the turtle.

Lutra looked in terror as something large moved just below the surface heading straight for the young seal. 'Saoirse! Saoirse!' the turtle yelled out a warning cry.

As the creature broke the surface behind the young seal,

Saoirse quickly turned to see the most hideous creature he had ever encountered. Lumps of skin were torn from the face. There was a large gaping socket where an eye should have been. Deep scars criss-crossed the face. Saoirse shrieked in terror and hurried over to the turtle for protection.

The grizzled old seal moved over to them. He opened his mouth, revealing a shattered upper jaw.

'What do you want?' Lutra asked nervously.

The seal found it difficult to speak and in slurred tones demanded food and shelter. Lutra hesitated for a moment then invited the seal to Grypus' island. 'There you will find shelter and we can supply food for you.'

The seal became calmer. He stared hard at Saoirse with his one good eye, then moved closer and sniffed him. Saoirse recoiled; the rank and musty odour of the seal's breath nearly made him retch.

'You are Saoirse, the son of Mara and Krail.'

Saoirse nodded nervously.

'I am Ri. I am from the same colony as your parents. I lived on the far side of the island.' His upper jaw began to bleed as he spoke. Saoirse remembered seeing him once in the water talking to his father and smiled faintly at him. 'It's good to see you, dear Saoirse. I thought I was the only one to survive the massacre.'

'I think we should head for the island,' Lutra said warmly.

* * *

'How dare you bring anyone onto my island, without my permission!' Grypus bellowed, as he watched the strange seal follow Lutra and Saoirse to the shore.

'Calm yourself,' said Lutra, easing himself onto the sandy shore.

'I will not have my hospitality taken for granted,' the old seal grumbled, as he pulled himself into a threatening posture.

The wounded seal gingerly came ashore. Grypus rushed at him with neck stretched out and mouth open wide. The stranger pulled himself into a defensive position. As Grypus got closer he suddenly stopped in his tracks. The sight of this poor wretched creature made him recoil in shock. He had never seen anything like those wounds on a living creature before. He wondered how the old seal had managed to survive.

'Please forgive the intrusion, but your friends kindly invited me here for food and shelter.'

'They did?' said Grypus, staring at Lutra and Saoirse. 'Well, of course you can stay. I would never turn away a kinsman if he's in trouble.'

'Thank you,' said the seal, then he coughed several times. Saliva and blood came from his mouth. Saoirse had to turn away at the sight.

The seal recovered himself and said weakly, 'My name is Ri. I'm from the same clan as young Saoirse.'

'Ri,' said Grypus. 'I knew your parents. They originally came from the coast of West Cork. Am I right?'

The seal nodded and a faint smile broke across his face.

'Go and bring over some fish,' said Grypus, 'to our friend here.'

Saoirse moved up to the rocks where Grypus kept a larder. He hurried back with a cod in his mouth.

'Perhaps you would be so kind as to tear it into smaller pieces for me. My jaw aches something terrible.'

'Of course,' said Grypus, taking the fish from Saoirse. Placing it under his left foreflipper he then began to tear small strips of the cod. They watched the seal try to eat the small morsels of fish. Every mouthful seemed to be very painful to swallow, but he persisted. It was an agony for the others to watch what a once strong powerful animal was reduced to.

'Must keep your strength up,' said Grypus awkwardly.

The seal rested after the food. In the evening he seemed a little stronger. The others huddled around him to shelter him from the chilly easterly winds that were blowing off the sea.

'I must look a sight,' said Ri. 'At least the darkness hides my grotesque features.'

'Nonsense,' said Grypus. 'You look fine.'

'I know only too well how I look. I saw myself in a rock pool. I didn't recognise myself.' Then he added with some irony, 'I'm still alive.'

'In a few weeks you will be back to your old self,' Grypus said cheerfully, 'when all those wounds heal up.'

'After what has happened, life has no meaning for me any more,' Ri said sadly.

The others stared in silence as he told them what had happened to the clan and the rookery. His eyes were in a trance as he relived the terrible events. Saoirse trembled as all the horrible images came flooding back into his own mind. Tears poured from Ri's good eye.

'The deathly silence that followed when the nusham had gone and the gulls had finished gorging on the flesh . . . I can remember picking my way over the bones of my family and friends . . . ' His face became contorted as he related the events. 'It was a dark time of murder and destruction,' he said grimly.

'Take it easy,' said the turtle.

The gentle voice jolted Ri out of the horror and made him realise where he was. He stared at the kind old face of Lutra. 'Sorry, I didn't mean to fill you with all that horror.'

'It's good to talk things out,' said the turtle.

'No good in bottling things up,' said Grypus.

'Are you all right, young Saoirse? You're a remarkable little fella,' said Ri. 'It does me good to see you, it gives me hope.'

'I think you should rest,' said Lutra.

'Yes, I'm so terribly tired.' He pulled himself behind a large boulder for shelter from the winds.

Grypus nuzzled Saoirse. 'I hope all that talk didn't upset you?'

'No,' said Saoirse, blinking back the tears.

'It's time we all rested. I'm flipper weary,' said Grypus.

Early next morning Saoirse hurried to see Ri, to ask him to go for a swim. He thought it might cheer him up. There sat Grypus and Lutra looking down at the fallen form of Ri. Blood was oozing from his gaping mouth.

Lutra looked at Saoirse. 'I'm afraid he's gone!'

Saoirse bleated softly.

'A happy release,' Grypus added sadly, as he looked upon Ri who was as still as the stones.

*   *   *

A flash of lightning illuminated the sea momentarily. Seafra could see the huddled shapes of the other seals on the rocks. The rain beat down hard as another fork of lightning tore along the black clouds. She bleated loudly but the pealing cries of birds drowned out her cry for help. The sudden storm had panicked the roosting birds as they wheeled around the inky sky.

The young seal desperately tried to get back to the island but the large waves buffeted her with such tremendous force that she was being pushed further and further away from her home

and family. All she could manage was to keep her head above the mass of water as the waves continued to sweep her away out into the vastness of the sea.

Seafra rolled over, making a slapping sound with her foreflippers which she hoped would echo through the water. With any luck one of her kin might be in the water searching for her at this very moment and would hear it. Seafra continued to slap her flippers with all her strength. She was getting more terrified as she moved through the dark waters.

Only a short time earlier she had been snuggling in to her mother, feeling her warm breath on her face. Seafra was dozing when the storm began. Why had she moved away from the security of her mother to investigate the strange light that touched the sea?

She didn't see the freak wave that swept her off the rocks into the water. Another great crashing and thundering in the sky panicked the young seal. She was suddenly swallowed up by the water. Down she slipped into the dark and silent deep.

Seafra somehow mustered some strength and struggled upwards. The sea was so tempestuous and violent that the waves grew up towards the sky. It seemed to the young seal that the sea and the sky were in a great rage with one another. Banks of black clouds continued to invade the sky. The winds churned up the water as the waves and currents continued to drag her away from her family.

The young seal was barely a week old. All she wanted was to be back with her kin on the island. Instead of that she was being pulled wherever the tides took her. She was chilled to the bone. Her white fur seemed unable to keep out the cold. It was a harsh introduction to life at sea for the young seal as she drifted in the deep valleys between the waves. She wondered if she could ride out the storm. It was something she couldn't answer. She could only give herself over to fate to decide whether she should live or die.

Chapter 5

Ben Reilly sat with a mug of hot tea reading the morning newspaper.

'More bad news,' he sighed. Sometimes he wondered why he read the newspapers. They were all filled with doom and gloom. It seemed the modern world was addicted to reading about man's inhumanity to man.

At sixty-seven years he was still a strong and relatively fit man, and in good health. Having spent most of his life building ships or sailing them he missed not doing that sort of work anymore. He was a bit of a work horse who enjoyed physical work, and thought he could keep going until he seized up. His one regret was that he did not get married and have a family.

But there again, he mused, a woman who could put up with him would have needed to be a saint. He laughed silently to himself and turned over several pages until he came to the sports section.

He was now living with his niece, Mary, and her two children, Justine and Deirdre. So in some ways he had his own family. He was very grateful indeed for their company.

Mary popped her head around the door. 'All right, Chappie?'

'Couldn't be better, sure haven't I the life of Reilly,' he laughed loudly.

'I'm off to town. Can I get you anything?'

'Well, if you could pick up a bit of tobacco and a few black pens.'

'Right. How's the book coming along?' she enquired.

'Slowly, very slowly. I have about the makings of four chapters so far.'

'That's great. We might have a best-seller out of you by Christmas,' she smiled warmly.

'I don't know which Christmas, maybe the year two thousand and twenty,' he laughed loudly.

'Well, I remember reading somewhere that James Joyce said to a friend he'd had a great day because he completed two sentences.'

'That's a good one all right, that gives me hope.' He sipped his tea then added. 'A book on boat-building is a far cry from a genius like Mr Joyce.'

Mary came over to him and put her arm around his shoulder and kissed him on the forehead. 'You're a genius to us.'

'God bless you, Mary. You have the gift of making everyone feel worthwhile.'

'Go away out of that,' she said cheerfully, heading for the door. 'Of course, I hope the genius will find time to finish those book shelves that were promised for the sitting room.'

'I'm not making excuses but I'm waiting for some sheets of elm that were promised to me from Harry in Dublin. I've stopped buying mahogany since I saw that programme about the destruction of the tropical rain forests.'

Mary put on her coat, then pulled a bobble from her red hair and shook her head several times. Her hair fell neatly from the crown in thick waves, framing her attractive face. 'I hope that's not an excuse,' she added with a twinkle.

'You have the word of a seafarer and you know a lie never comes from their lips,' he winked.

'Listen, I'm away,' said Mary. 'Can I get you a refill before I go?'

'Off with you,' said Chappie. 'I'll manage a second cup of tea on my own.'

'The girls are on the beach – they'll probably come in starving. There's cold meat and cheese in the fridge and I've made some fresh brown bread and soup for you all.'

'That's great,' said Chappie. 'Now you take your time and I'll have the potatoes and vegetables ready by the time you get back.'

'Oh, that would be great. I think I'll get my hair cut while I'm in Wexford.'

Chappie watched her through the window as she drove away down the drive. How could any man leave such a lovely woman like that he wondered. His thoughts returned to the night she and the two children had turned up on the doorstep of his cottage, having just flown in from Boston. 'It's over,' she had sobbed, 'between Jeff and me.' That was over four years ago, he recalled.

Chappie never asked what had happened to cause the break-up of their marriage and she never said. Nor did she ever say an unkind word about Jeff, her ex-husband.

He remembered the wedding so well. It was he who gave the bride away in the church, since her parents had died three years earlier. His poor brother had been so devastated at the death of his wife, he knew he would be following her shortly afterwards. He remembered one of the village women saying that before the year was out his brother would be with her. It was truly a case of a broken heart.

The only time he spoke to Mary's husband after the break-up was one evening when Jeff phoned from Seattle. Mary was out at one of her evening classes. He said to tell her the divorce papers had come through. When pressed as to why this had happened, he simply said that people grow apart. 'I guess we got bored with each other.'

It took all Ben Reilly's patience not to give him a piece of his mind and challenge him about his flippant remark. You can get bored with a TV programme or a book. But to get bored with such a beautiful woman as his dear niece, he just couldn't fathom.

Still, he had no right to judge. He knew very few people really meet their soul mates in this world. All he said to Jeff was: 'I'm sorry to hear it didn't work out, but I'll pass on the message.'

'That's life,' Jeff said casually, and hung up.

Ben Reilly felt how trite his own remark was on that occasion. He picked up his mug, headed to the kitchen and lifted the teapot to give himself a refill. Then he returned to his favourite chair and took up the paper again.

His thoughts floated back to the time they all lived in his tiny fishing cottage, and then Mary bought an old farmhouse with twelve acres near Curracloe. He was delighted to be asked if he would come and live with them. With the sale of his own cottage he was able to finance the new roof that needed to be put on the old farmhouse, and the re-wiring of it. The rest of the work he managed to do himself.

Mary had the touch to turn a damp, cold, old farmhouse into a charming home for them. At thirty-three she had not lost any of her beauty or determination. Starting teaching again in the local primary school as a part-time teacher, it wasn't long before she'd got a permanent position. She was happy to be living back home again.

He filled his pipe with the last of his tobacco from the pouch and lit it. Sitting back deeply into the armchair he sucked on the pipe, then slowly blue smoke began to leak from between his lips.

He turned to the sound of the children's voices as they moved past the sitting-room window. They hurried in the back door, through the kitchen, then burst into the room, panting hard. He raised his eyes over the newspaper and gazed at them gently. They stood together pulling at their jackets trying to recover from their long run up from the beach.

'Where's the fire?' he asked, mockingly.

They hurried to him and started to pull him out of the armchair.

'Quick, Chappie. We need to show you something right away.' Justine and Deirdre tried to pull their grand-uncle from the chair.

'Steady on, steady on. I can manage, girls. This must be something very important for you to disturb your old Chappie from enjoying his favourite pipe.' He got up, put his pipe in the ashtray and gulped down some of the tea.

'Oh please hurry,' said Justine. 'Here's your jacket, and your stick.' They helped him into his jacket and handed him his carved stick.

'What's all the fuss about?' he asked as they ushered him out the back door.

'It's something very exciting,' said Deirdre.

'You won't believe it,' said Justine.

'What will I not believe?' he asked, as they opened the farm gate and led him along the narrow dirt track towards the beach. 'Are you going to keep me in suspense all day?' he asked as he began to pant.

'It's a surprise. You'll see,' said Deirdre.

'It's deadly,' Justine exclaimed.

'Well, I hope it's not too deadly,' he smiled, as they made their way over the sand dunes and down the steep slopes towards the beach. A kestrel hovered up ahead searching the dunes for insects. He stopped and pointed to the sky. 'Look girls, it's a . . . '

'Quickly,' interrupted Justine. 'It's not far now.'

He almost slipped several times as he made his way down the dunes. A skylark planed up into the air and hovered momentarily before returning back into the marram grass. As the two girls hurried to the water's edge, a cormorant lifted from the water, feet and wings working furiously to take off. With frantic flight it sped away low over the waves.

'It was right here, honest,' said Justine, looking very disappointed.

'Yes,' said Deirdre. 'I remember that piece of driftwood with the seaweed on it.'

Chappie began to get his breath back as he straightened up. 'What was here?' he demanded to know, resting his full weight on his walking stick. The two girls looked up and down the empty beach. 'Is this some kind of a wild goose chase to trick your old Chappie from enjoying his morning paper?'

'No,' said Justine. 'Honest. It really was here.'

'For the umpteenth time,' he said in exasperated tones, 'what was here?

'There! Look! There it is,' Deirdre pointed, jumping up and down with excitement.

The young seal had broken the surface of the water to gulp a breath. She raised her torso and stared at the nusham on the beach to assess whether they would prove to be a danger or not.

At first Chappie didn't see it behind the white surf, then he spotted it. 'Ah, I see,' he exclaimed pointing with his stick.

A big roller covered the seal. It began splashing in panic in the clear emerald water. Seafra bleated loudly. Then a large growling breaker washed her to the shore.

'Poor thing, she looks bedraggled and sea tossed,' said Chappie as he moved over to the young seal. The girls bent over to pet her.

'Don't!' bellowed Chappie in a stern voice. He was now standing above the seal pup. 'It might bite.' He finished the sentence.

'What will we do?' asked Justine.

'It looks lost. We can't leave it here,' added Deirdre.

Chappie looked out to sea but could see no sign of its mother, or any seals for that matter.

'Look' said Justine, pointing to something far out to sea. 'That long black shape.'

Chappie stared hard, then realised it was a flock of ducks lazily floating in between the heaving waves. 'That's a flock of common scoters. They look like a raft on the water.'

The young seal barked. Chappie bent over looking into the moist eyes of the pup and said warmly. 'Are you lost? Has your mother abandoned you?' Seafra lay spread-eagled along the tideline. 'Listen, girls. Its mother might be nearby watching us and is waiting for us to move away before she comes to it. Or else it is abandoned.'

'We can't leave it here,' said Justine. 'It might die. It's probably very hungry.'

Chappie scratched his chin. 'We could sit for a time in the dunes and watch from a safe distance to see if the mother returns and make sure no dog attacks it or any crows or gulls start pecking at it.'

'Oh let's . . . please,' pleaded Justine.

'Okay,' said Chappie. 'But if you start to get cold we better go back for our coats. Besides, your mother won't be back until late afternoon.'

They sat patiently watching the young seal from the sand dunes. There was no one on the beach other than themselves. Chappie reckoned they would need to wait at least four hours. He pulled up his collar and adjusted his cap to get it to cover as much of his head as possible. A chilly wind blew over the dunes sending sand particles into their faces and eyes.

'What time is it?' asked Deirdre, stretching her legs and adjusting her position.

'We've been waiting over an hour so far,' said Chappie.

'It's lovely,' said Justine. 'How old do you think it is?'

'Hard to say,' Chappie answered, offering them some Silvermints which he took from the top pocket of his jacket. 'I think they lose their white fur after they're three weeks old. I read that somewhere or saw it on one of those interesting wildlife programmes.'

'So it's about a week or two old,' Justine added.

'That's about right.' It was lovely to see their faces, Chappie mused, when they set eyes upon the young seal. The children were helping him to look again at the world with young eyes. Then his thoughts darkened. He reckoned the pup hadn't been weaned by the mother yet. He had no idea how to care for this poor little creature. He only hoped the mother would turn up soon, otherwise he felt the young seal pup would be doomed.

*　*　*

Mary Wayne arrived home in the late afternoon and entered through the back door. 'Hi, I'm home,' she hollered cheerfully.

The house seemed unusually quiet. Normally she would hear the television blasting out from the sitting room where the children would be watching it. Or Chappie playing some of his favourite opera records or listening to the radio, or even snoring in the armchair. She looked over to the worktable. No sign of any potatoes peeled. That was unusual because if Chappie promised to do something he would do it. They must be out for a walk, she assumed.

Taking off her coat, she began to prepare the dinner. Two hours later there was still no sign of her uncle or the children. She was now becoming anxious. He would normally leave a note saying if he was staying away late. She put their meals on a plate in a warm oven.

Perhaps she should phone Margaret, her neighbour who lived a half a mile away. The children went to play there quite often. Chappie too was no stranger to the O'Haras' house. He would spend hours chatting to Margaret's father. And when they got into heavy discussion about politics, religion or the sea, they would forget time and argue and debate into the night.

Mary picked up the phone and was about to dial the number when she heard an unearthly sound outside. It startled her, it sounded just like someone being tortured. The back door opened, Mary picked up the poker and held it tightly in her right hand. Then she heard the sound of the children.

'Mammy, you wouldn't believe what we found on the beach,' Deirdre exclaimed.

'I was getting worried about you.'

Justine pulled at her arm. 'It's lovely. Come and see.'

'What's lovely? You're freezing cold,' she scolded Justine. 'Where is Chappie?' she demanded to know, placing her arms on her hips.

'Just outside . . . at the shed.'

'If your dinner is all dried up you have only yourself to blame.'

Chappie entered the kitchen. He had a very sheepish look on his face.

Mary stared at him. 'You look like a cat who has just swallowed the pet canary.'

'Now, Mary dear, just like your mother. You can read me like a book . . .'

'What is it you're hiding in the shed?' she asked flatly.

'It's a baby seal,' said Justine. 'Come and see.' Justine took her mother by the hand and hustled her out to the shed. Chappie and Deirdre followed. Chappie had picked up a torch from the kitchen shelf and shone it on the seal pup. The seal looked up and sneezed.

'Ah, the poor thing,' said Mary, picking bits of seaweed from its white fur. 'What can we do with you, you poor little mite? I wonder can we give it milk . . . ?' She looked at Chappie.

'I don't know, perhaps some water and give it a chance to settle down.' Chappie closed the shed door leaving the young seal bleating.

'Let's put it in the bath,' Deirdre suggested.

'I don't think that's a good idea. You lot come in for your dinner and I'll try to contact the warden on the reserve, or the wildlife ranger. They're sure to know what to do,' declared Mary.

She phoned the Wexford Wildfowl Reserve, but the warden was out bird ringing, so she left a message on the answering machine. She phoned the wildlife ranger who was out on patrol and left a message for him with all the details on his answering machine. There wasn't much more she could do. Blackie, their border collie, began to bark and scratch at the shed door. The seal started to wail loudly.

'So much for a quiet evening and a soak in the bath,' she sighed.

'Can we keep it?' Deirdre asked.

'No, dear!' said Mary. 'It belongs in the wild and we cannot keep it here, I'm sorry.' The girls looked disappointed.

'Your mother is right. As soon as it is ready we will have to return it to the sea. In the meantime . . . '

Mary smiled. 'It can stay, the weekend only!'

'Wait till I tell all my friends in school,' said Justine.

Mary had visions of the entire school turning up on their doorstep wanting to see the seal.

That evening, the wildlife ranger, Pat Buckley, was the first to arrive to the house. Then the warden, Bob Shackleton, came shortly afterwards. Chappie brought them out to see the seal which was resting on some old hessian sacks.

Mary began to make some tea for her visitors and had anticipated their calling by producing a freshly baked apple tart. Just as they sat down to have their supper of hot apple tart and ice cream, there was the sound of another jeep pulling up outside the front door. Blackie barked loudly. There was a heavy knock on the door. Chappie hurried over to open the door.

'Is this . . . ?'

Before he could finish his sentence Chappie had ushered in the stranger. 'No need to guess who this man is,' Chappie smiled, pointing at the man's sweatshirt with Seal Rescue blazoned across it.

The man smiled broadly and introduced himself as Bill Fortune. Mary took his jacket and asked the girls to get him some tea and tart.

'Thank you for coming down at such short notice,' said Mary.

'Oh, it's a twenty-four hour service,' he beamed. 'The sanctuary is only two hours from Wexford. I normally end up rushing to Dingle or Malin Head. This is a doddle,' he grinned, taking the tea and tart from Justine. Bill Fortune was a younger man than his wild grey beard and dishevelled hair might suggest. He had powerful hands which showed a few recent cuts and scars.

He was well acquainted with Bob Shackleton and Pat Buckley, having been involved with them in other seal rescues, as well as the treatment of oiled sea birds. Chappie filled his pipe and admitted it was the first time, even with all his years at sea, he'd had a seal pup so close.

After supper Bill Fortune checked the seal. It was thin for its age but it had no sign of any physical injury. Heavy rain began to fall on the corrugated roof of the shed. Chappie suggested they should stay the night and Bill could head back to Dublin in the morning. Pat and Bob declined the kind invitation, since they lived nearby, but would love another cup of tea. Pat smiled broadly.

'Nothing stronger?' Mary asked.

'Oh no thanks,' said Pat. 'I'm on duty tomorrow. I need a clear head,' he laughed.

'It's nearly bedtime for you two madams,' said Mary.

'Please can we stay up a little longer? We want to find out all about seals,' Justine pleaded.

'I'm sure Mr. Fortune is exhausted after his long journey.'

'I've something to show you girls,' Bill Fortune declared, as he sat back into the sofa and took out some photographs he had in his wallet. The girls leaned over the sofa and Bill explained the pictures. 'This is Sinbad, he's a common seal, more snub-nosed than the grey seal pup you are minding. The common seal is smaller than the Atlantic grey seal.' The pictures were passed around.

Chappie put on his glasses. 'What are these?' pointing at two seals in a pool.

'Male and female grey seals, the male is bigger than the female. More of a thick neck and shoulders.' Mary could see how much Bill was devoted to these sea mammals. 'These mammals are like you and me,' he pointed to Deirdre. Deirdre looked quite surprised. 'They're warm-blooded, air breathing, but unlike us they spend most of the time in the water.'

'I spend a lot of time in the water,' said Deirdre. 'Especially during the summer.' They all laughed.

Bill sipped his fresh cup of tea. 'They don't have hands like us but they have flippers – the foreflippers in front and the hind flippers which point backwards.'

'What's a pack of seals called?' Chappie asked, enjoying the conversation.

'Well, they're called a herd, like cattle – the female is a cow and the male is a bull.'

'Then the pup should be called a calf,' said Justine.

'True,' agreed Bill. 'But it's known as a pup.'

'How long can they stay under water?' Justine asked.

'Seals can stay under water up to thirty minutes.'

'Steady on,' said Mary. 'He's not a walking encyclopaedia.'

Bill smiled and gulped some more tea.

'Thirsty work, all this interrogating,' laughed Chappie.

'The fur seal is the smallest,' said Bill, 'if my memory serves me correctly.'

'What could have happened to this baby seal?' Mary enquired.

'Well, it may have been washed off-shore by a freak wave,

these things can happen. Or maybe the mother was killed or injured.'

'There's a seal colony at Raven's Point,' said Pat Buckley. 'Chances are it's from there.'

'How do you manage to feed a young pup that hasn't been weaned by its mother?' Bob enquired.

'A lamb tube-feeder does the job, and that would be filled with lactade which is a mixture of sugar, salt and water. My local vet has become an expert in dealing with seals since I've moved there,' he grinned. 'Before it was dogs and cats, now he has to handle big powerful seals, some suffering from pneumonia or pleurisy, eye infections, nasal discharge, bites and tears to the body. You name it, he's had to treat it. And of course you need gloves when handling these seals. They can give you a savage bite.' Bill scratched his beard and said softly, 'I've studied seals for years from a welfare and scientific viewpoint, and they still retain some mystery for me. They're fascinating creatures.'

Bob Shackleton turned to the young girls. 'Of course, there are many legends relating to seals.'

'Please can we hear them,' Justine pleaded. Mary looked at the clock. It was 9.45 pm. 'Girls, it's very late.'

'Oh please,' said Deirdre.

'Well, since it's not every night we have such distinguished company . . . '

'Thanks a million, Mammy,' said the girls in unison. They moved on the floor and sat looking up at the four men.

'Some people,' said Bob Shackleton in low sinister tones, 'believe seals are the souls of drowned sailors.' The two girls hugged each other. 'Others,' he continued, 'believe there are creatures called Selchies. These are men, women and children you might see playing at the water's edge. If you get close to them you will see their clothes on the sand above the tideline. But . . . ' he took a deep breath, took off his spectacles, hawed on the glass and cleaned them with a part of his cotton shirt.

'What?' Justine urged him to continue.

'If you look carefully at their clothes you will discover they are not clothes at all, but seal fur coats. After a time these humans will climb back into the seal coats and return to the sea.' The girls looked wide eyed. 'Sometimes,' Bob continued, 'if you manage to get up close to these "people", you will see some tell-tale signs that they are seal people.'

'What signs?' asked Justine.

'Their hands and feet are partly webbed. Some people don't even know they are "Selchies". There are clues, of course. They love the sea and they play a lot on the sand.'

'We love the sea,' said Deirdre nervously.

Justine and Deirdre checked their own hands to see if there was any webbing on them.

The men laughed loudly. Bill Fortune remembered a legend he had read or heard about. Again the girls begged to hear it. The mother said this was definitely the last story before bedtime.

Bill folded his arms and took a deep breath. 'Once upon a time there was a king of Norway, which was called Lochlann in those days. He had a beautiful wife and three children and he lived in a lovely castle beside the sea. Sadly one day his beautiful wife fell from her horse and died. The king was broken hearted, and of course the children were very sad too. Then a year or two passed and the king's advisors suggested he should get himself a new queen for the sake of the kingdom and the children.

'A second marriage was arranged for the king. His new queen was a beautiful but cold-hearted woman who was also skilled in the practice of the black arts.'

'What's that?' Deirdre interrupted.

'Black magic!' said her mother, who was becoming a little anxious that this story would cause nightmares for her eight and nine-year old daughters.

Bill noticed the expression on their mother's face and so began to simplify the story as he related it. 'The wicked step-mother became jealous of the attention the king showered on his children, so one night the queen made a magic potion which she slipped into the children's food. Then she took them down to the seashore for a walk. No sooner had they touched the water's edge than the three children turned into grey seals and hurried out into the wild sea never to be seen again.'

'It is said that their offspring must return to the land at least three times a year to walk the lonely shores. There they will take off the seal skins and become human. But they have no desire to stay on dry land. Sometimes people steal their fur coats and they cannot return to the sea. This makes them very lonely and sad. Some say they become sailors or seafarers.'

'That must be what happened to me,' said Chappie, tossing Justine's hair.

'That's a very sad story,' said Justine. 'I hope the seal pup we found isn't a Sel . . . '

'Selchie,' said her mother.

'I don't know,' said Bob.

'That's why it's important we get her back to the sea,' Pat added.

'It's time to get you to bed,' said Mary. The girls kissed their grand-uncle goodnight, shook hands with the other three men, kissed their Mam and hurried to their bedroom.

Mary called after them, 'Light out, no talking, don't forget to brush your teeth and sweet dreams.'

'Maybe we should all make a move home,' said Pat.

'No hurry', said Mary. 'It's a bad old night. You are all welcome to stay the night, there's plenty of room.'

The men were rather comfortable sitting beside the warm fire and chatting away. Pat pulled out his mobile phone and phoned his wife to tell her he'd be home late. Bob did the same thing. Chappie slipped out to the kitchen and returned with several cans of Guinness.

'Sure you might as well settle down and relax. It's Saturday night and if we talk sweetly to Mary we might get a song out of her.'

Without any coaxing Chappie sang a few sea shanties before finally persuading his niece to sing a few of his old favourite Irish ballads. Chappie regaled them with stories from the sea. Pat told some amusing stories relating to his work as a wildlife ranger. Bob gave some interesting insights into the facts and the folklore of birds.

Mary finally got to bed after two o'clock. She hadn't laughed or enjoyed an evening so much for years. She was always organising and planning her life, yet she was reminded that evening that it's important to let things happen in life as well. She recalled reading that Renoir once said that he liked to be a cork and to float on the sea of life. Maybe all the planning prevents the fates from entering into one's life, she mused.

Through the floorboards she could hear the men still laughing and chatting downstairs. Mary said a quiet prayer in the darkness for all those gentle souls who try to do their best in life. She had met her fair share of ruthless people who were always taking, never giving.

Tears filled her eyes. Most of the time she managed to keep her feelings and emotions well under control but tonight there was a heightened awareness of things she couldn't explain. It was as if all her feelings were finely tuned and open to all. Perhaps it was because of looking into the eyes of that little wild orphan as if they were keys to unlock her feelings. She'd never prayed for a wild creature before but tonight she prayed not only for her children but also for that poor helpless white furred seal that slept in the old shed.

Early next morning after breakfast, Mary, Chappie and the children watched Bill Fortune place the seal pup into a wicker basket and then into his jeep. He promised he would keep them informed about the progress of the seal. 'If it does survive,' he whispered into Chappie's ear, 'I will return it to the wild on the beach at Curracloe.' Chappie shook his hand warmly.

Bill presented the children with a poster all about seals. He thanked Mary for her hospitality, then let Justine and Deirdre have one last look at the seal before he departed.

Chapter 6

The water rippled gently to the shore. Three heads could be seen bobbing just above the surface as they made their way to the island.

It had been a good day. Grypus had the gift of finding the "hot spots" where the shoals of mackerel would be. There was time for games, which Saoirse enjoyed. And time to find out more about his environment.

He was now able to identify the different birds as well as the fish and other strange creatures that inhabited the world of water, like sea cucumbers, sea anemones, urchins, starfish, jellyfish, and even coral. He was a good student who had a hunger for knowledge and old Grypus and Lutra were only too willing to pass on their knowledge and wisdom.

Saoirse had lost his barrel shape and was more streamlined, with sleek brown speckled fur.

'I'm flipper weary,' said Grypus, as he struggled to pull his heavy frame up the beach to the rocks. Saoirse was exhausted too, but he didn't feel the least bit sleepy.

Earlier they had visited the big island where the nusham lived. He saw the sea stacks which the cormorants used to rear their young, the cliffs that were home to kittiwakes, fulmars, guillemots, choughs, razorbills, great black-backed gulls, herring gulls and lesser black-backed gulls – all of whom share the cliffs during the breeding seasons.

Saoirse remembered the dizzy sensation of looking up along these sheer cliffs. And Grypus explained how the great forces of sea and wind had shaped them. Every part was beaten and scoured by the elements. Now the crevices and ledges are used

by the birds to lay their eggs and then raise their young.

'Sometimes the ledges crumble and large chunks can fall away into the sea. So you be careful, young fella,' he added in serious tones.

Saoirse wriggled ashore, looked once over his shoulder and smiled as Lutra hauled himself out of the water. Then the three of them looked at the star-filled sky. There was a ring around the silver moon.

'It's time you had a lesson about these strange lights in the dark velvet sky.' Saoirse nodded and nuzzled Lutra. 'Pay attention,' said the turtle as he gazed upon the celestial canopy. 'Our ancestors believed that the stars were the ancient ones watching over us, making sure we live our lives in accordance with Mother Nature. They expect us to be great fires and to light up the world in a special caring way. Not to be like little puffs of smoke that vanish without a trace. They know we sometimes have to kill to eat, but we must be always grateful to the fish or eel that gives up its life for us. We should ask the ancient ones to allow these creatures to return again to live, breed and continue to flourish as a species.'

'Do nusham do this after they kill our kind?' Saoirse asked.

Grypus interjected. 'I think the nusham have forgotten, or turned their backs on the ancient ones. They certainly act like they have,' he grumbled. 'Always killing far more than they need to. They hate us, you know, because they see us as competition. I think they might be even envious of the way we can swim, catch our food and stay under water for such a long period.'

'But there are lots of fish in the sea,' Saoirse offered. 'Enough for all.'

'Not if the nusham continue to fish out the seas,' Grypus continued. 'As they have been doing since I was a pup. Soon there will be empty seas if they don't leave the fish alone during the breeding seasons.'

'Let's change the subject,' said Lutra. 'You know how much it upsets you.'

Grypus snorted and scratched his torso. 'Tell young Saoirse more about those bright lights we call stars.'

Lutra cleared his throat and raised his head. 'Like us, the stars like to wander. They move from the southern skies to set in the western horizon, while more and more rise in the east. Some say it's our world that moves, not the sky at all, and you know, Saoirse, after all these years travelling the world I'm beginning to believe this.'

'Now, you see that nice pattern of stars above Grypus' head? That's called the Great Bear inside that constellation. That shape is the Dipper, the gulls call it the Plough because it reminds them of when the nusham tear up the fields with a thing called a plough. The black-headed gulls love the nusham's plough for they swoop down and eat all the worms, grubs and insects that are disturbed by it. To continue, follow the handle of the Plough to the two outer stars . . . have you got that?' Lutra enquired.

Saoirse moved along the star pattern with his eyes. 'Yes, I've got them.'

'Good,' said Lutra. 'Now look up from them high into the sky in a straight line, you will see a star called the Pole Star or sometimes called Polaris. That star has guided me many a time during my night journeying for it always remains in the same place. Now, turn your eyes to those three stars in the southern sky.'

Saoirse finally located them. 'I see them,' he said excitedly. 'They're just like us, resting in the dark.'

Grypus chuckled quietly.

'Yes,' said Lutra. 'Just like us. That is called the belt of Orion. Now, turn your eyes to the left and a little below you will see a very bright star called Sirius. In fact, it is the brightest star in the whole sky. Now, see the misty patches of light?'

Saoirse couldn't see anything only stars, then he finally could make out a vague misty cloud. 'I see,' said Saoirse 'very faintly.'

'That's called Nebula. Squint your eyes and you should make out a river of stars. That is called The Milky Way.'

'Wow!' said the young seal in awe.

'So young Saoirse, you need never feel alone or lonely, for the stars will always be there for you.'

'Oh, I'll never feel lonely because I have Grypus and you. You are my stars.'

Chapter 7

Seafra began to be relaxed and calm in her new surroundings.

She had felt bouts of nausea after the long journey, but these had passed. She had been taken from the wicker basket and placed in a small holding pool where she splashed about and stretched her tired stiff body. It felt so good to be back in water even though this water was different from what she was used to; it wasn't deep, just enough water for her to submerge in and still keep her nostrils out of the water. This water even tasted good. She lapped it up and slaked her thirst.

Birds she had never seen before wandered on the lawn. She saw large black birds whose plumage shimmered when the morning sun shone across their backs. They had strong heavy bills with which they hammered the ground and were occasionally rewarded with a grub or worm. There were other more cheeky birds which appeared – black and white with long tails. They rattled away in annoyance at her presence. Seafra just stared back and submerged her body.

They picked at the remains of fish that had been discarded alongside another larger pool. A small bird with an orange breast flew to the edge of a twig on a holly bush and sang a few clear notes. Seafra liked the soothing sound of the robin's song certainly a lot better than the noise of the magpies that had by now flown high into a chestnut tree.

Seafra heard a door opening and closing, then a footfall on the gravel. 'Time for your breakfast, young lady.' The voice seemed friendly and calm. Seafra recognised the man and knew the scent. Suddenly she was lifted clear out of the water by her hind flippers. She bleated loudly and wailed as the man placed her on a blanket. 'Take it easy, girlie.'

He straddled her, then rubbed the sides of her face. Seafra felt a thin object passing over her tongue and moving down her throat. She struggled furiously. The man stroked her gently as the liquid food travelled into her stomach. Seafra shook her head trying to resist, but the more liquid poured into her the less she struggled. She realised this nusham didn't want to harm her, but she didn't know what he was up to either.

A black cat padded across the garden and began to rub against the man, her tail twisting and turning. 'Hello, Ebony. Have you met Lady?' The cat purred, then clawed at his jumper. 'I'll get your breakfast in a minute.' He smiled, pushing the cat gently away. A rooster passed sure-footed across the lawn and made a low rumbling sound. 'Everyone will get their breakfast as soon as we feed our new guest.' A large collie came bounding out and jumped up behind Bill Fortune, nearly unbalancing him. 'Steady on, Brandy. I'm nearly through.' The man stood up and stretched his tired body, gave a loud yawn, then stretched his arms as high as he could into the air.

Bending over, he stroked the seal. 'You'll do well, I can tell. This afternoon we'll get James, the vet, to check you over. In the meantime you might as well get familiar with your new home.' Seafra watched the man walk away, followed by the dog and cat. Then she heard a door opening and closing.

The rooks returned to feed on the lawn, while the geese and hens made their way into the field beyond the garden. Her gnawing pangs of hunger were gone. She lay there, watching. She had never seen so many strange creatures before.

Back at the rookery, apart from her kind, only the occasional sea bird floated overhead. When she thought of the rookery she began to feel very lonely. Up to now most of her feelings had ranged from confusion to sheer terror. Now, this new sensation of loss seemed more painful than any of the other feelings. She covered her head with one of her foreflippers and tried to remember her mother's face and the other members of her family. Then she remembered being tossed about by the furious surf that night. This panicked her and she wailed loudly.

'Take it easy now,' said a gentle voice that sounded vaguely familiar. Seafra raised her head. A whiskery face was staring at her. It was one of her own kind, yet different. 'When did you arrive?' the stranger enquired.

'This morning,' said Seafra. 'Who are you?'

'I'm Tang. I've been here over two full moons.'

'Are you one of us? You look different,' said Seafra.

'Well, if you mean am I a seal, well of course I am. I'm a common seal. I take it you haven't seen one like me before?'

'No,' said Seafra.

'Well, we're known as the snub noses. Your lot have a longer muzzle, and you grow bigger than us. But apart from that we're more or less the same.'

'What happened to your fur, you're all patchy?' Seafra enquired.

'Well, for one so young you're very observant, and very pass remarkable. I'm in a moult actually. It happens at this time of the year. It will happen to you too, young lady. That white baby fur will soon be replaced by a warmer tighter fur. It's nothing to worry about, all perfectly natural. Where are you from?' Tang enquired.

'I'm from County Wexford.'

'Oh I've been there, stayed for a while near Hook Head. I

suppose you want to know where I'm from? A place called Malin Head in County Donegal. It's wild and beautiful.'

'I would like to travel around the big island,' said Seafra. 'My mother told me many stories about places she had visited.'

'How did you end up here?' Tang wondered.

'Well, I don't really know. One minute I'm with my family sitting out a raging storm, next thing a wave washes over me and I'm dragged into the sea in the dark.'

'You poor thing. You must have been terrified,' Tang said.

'I was. I felt like a piece of kelp being tossed about for hours. Next thing I knew I was on a beach being stared at by two nusham pups.'

'They're called children actually,' Tang interjected.

'Then I was brought to their cave.'

'You mean a house.'

'Yes,' said Seafra. 'A house. Later a man came and brought me here. Is he going to eat us?' Seafra asked nervously.

The common seal chuckled. 'No, of course not. This nusham is kind and I have it from a good authority, a common gull to be precise, that when we seals are strong and healthy the nusham brings us back to our home in the sea.'

'Can you believe the gull?' Seafra asked.

'For one so young you are very cagey,' Tang smiled. 'The common gull in question arrived here with a wing injury. The nusham could easily have fed it to the cat but he didn't. He looked after the gull until its wing was mended. It was released at the seashore. It came back several times to say 'hello'. When two grey seals were being returned to the sea, the gull agreed to follow the nusham and see whether he was truly returning them to the water or doing something worse.'

'What do you mean?' Seafra interrupted.

'Well, seals may not be eaten by nusham in these parts, but some have been . . . ' she whispered in Seafra's ear, '. . . skinned!' Seafra recoiled in horror. 'Then the skin is made into a coat for other nusham.'

Seafra was sorry she had asked.

'As I said, not around here . . . in a different country it happens.' Tang continued to relate how the common gull had watched the nusham drive to a wide open beach and release the seals back into the waters. There were many other nusham looking on and not trying to stop them escaping.

'Will that happen to us?' Seafra asked.

'I'm certain of it.'

Seafra became more relaxed, knowing that no matter how long her stay here, someday she would get her freedom. In the meantime as long as she was being fed, cared for and had good company like Tang, things wouldn't be too bad.

*   *   *

When the sun was directly above Seafra, the nusham came over to her again. This time he had another nusham with him. Again Seafra was taken from her holding pool and placed on a blanket, while the two men examined her. Seafra instinctively lashed out, trying to bite the nusham.

'She's a lively one,' laughed Bill. 'Now you see why I wear these thick gloves.'

The vet continued his examination. Bill prised open the mouth of the pup and the vet examined inside 'Phew . . . bad breath,' he grimaced. 'Next time my wife complains about my heavy breath I'll bring her to smell this.'

Seafra's eyes were gently flushed with clean sea water. The smell of the sea water in Seafra's nostrils made her homesick. The men held her tightly and fed her again.

She was force-fed every four hours. It wasn't a patch on mother's milk, but Seafra felt good after each feed. Over the next few days she was fed and weighed. She was then moved to a bigger pool where she could swim about with her friend, Tang.

Tang loved talking and regaling Seafra with stories about other seals and animals that had been in the sanctuary for a time. The dog had become used to Seafra and had stopped barking very time she hauled herself out of the pool. The cat ignored her totally, the geese occasionally pulled at her fur. Sometimes early in the morning or in the late afternoon, a grey heron would come and visit the garden. It was mainly to pick up any fish left over from Tang who was a messy eater. Sometimes Tang would swallow the fish whole, tail first, other times she just bit into the fish. The nusham seemed to be very generous with the fish for he nearly always gave her more than she could possibly eat in a day. The heron's sharp eye missed none of the discarded fish. It too left the sanctuary well-fed.

On one frosty night Seafra saw a ghostly white bird flitting over the meadow, hovering for a time, then slipping away on soft hushed wings. The dog explained it was a barn owl out hunting for mice. Sometimes the owl gave out a strangled shriek which always startled Seafra. The dog claimed that the sound from young seal pups was infinitely worse.

One morning the nusham came to Seafra carrying a black bucket full of herring and sprat. 'Well, my little lady, it's time we tried you on some whole fish.' Seafra had been fed for the past few days on liquidised herring and additives, so she was aware of the taste of the fish but not sure whether she could manage a whole one. The man straddled her, tickled the sides of her cheek, and as she opened her mouth he pushed the fish in, tail first.

Seafra wriggled furiously tossing her head from side to side, trying to regurgitate the herring. But the man seemed determined to force-feed her. She gulped it down, then another one was forced into her mouth. This time she put up less of a struggle and swallowed the sprat without much difficulty.

After several fish the nusham released her and smiled down at her. 'Good girlie, you're well on the way to recovery.' He went over to Tang and lifted her by her hind flippers before she had a chance to get into the big pool. Tang snorted and barked as the nusham weighed her. 'A hundred and twenty pounds. You're a good weight,' he beamed, then returned her to the large pool.

*   *   *

Tang and Seafra sat huddled together. It was an exceptionally cold night. The dog was asleep in his kennel and the cat was sleeping in the nusham house. Tang explained that a grey seal's mother would encourage her offspring to make their own way in life once they were three weeks old, and since Seafra was now well into her fourth week she must be strong and independent and be prepared to fend for herself and perhaps wander the seas alone.

Seafra wondered why Tang was speaking like this since she could not leave the sanctuary. Besides, she enjoyed the common seal's company and didn't want to be alone. Tang sensed Seafra's anxiety but explained that life was constantly changing and that things might be different when she returned to the seas.

Hushy, the barn owl, alighted on a post and preened for a

time. 'Night peace to you,' she said in warm tones.

The seals returned the greeting.

'Nights are getting colder,' said the owl, ruffling its feathers.

'Yes, very cold,' said Tang.

'Sad about Greybell,' she sighed.

'Greybell?' wondered Tang.

'The grey heron,' said the owl. 'Killed the other evening.'

'How?' asked Seafra.

'It accidentally flew into the new wires the nusham put across the meadow. Killed instantly,' said the owl sadly.

Although they had never known the heron by name or even spoken to her they certainly would miss her around. Tang had often grumbled when her fish had been taken, but now she regretted not having been more friendly to the heron when she had come calling.

'Well, I'm away,' said the owl, and lifted from the post and glided away.

'That's what you mean by things changing,' said Seafra.

Tang's eyes moistened over. 'Yes!'

*   *   *

The sound of an engine rumbling startled Seafra. Bleary-eyed she turned to see where the noise was coming from. The jeep had moved from the nusham house and was heading along the gravel drive. It stopped near the large pool. Jackdaws and rooks left from the lawn with a clatter and headed over the trees to the far fields.

The jeep began to reverse over the grass, and stopped at the edge of the large pool. Tang, who was porpoising up and down the pool, suddenly stopped and watched as the two nusham got out of the jeep and walked to the back of the vehicle. She submerged herself completely as they lifted out a large wicker basket and placed it near the edge of the pool.

'I knew she'd do that,' said Bill. 'They always sense it.' He pulled on his wellies and then his gloves and began to wade out into the pool. Seafra barked as loudly as she could but no one took any notice.

'Gotcha!' said Bill as he began to pull Tang by the hind flippers out of the water. The other man tilted over the box, holding up the lid. When Bill got the common seal on the lawn, he towelled her down, taking off any excess water. Tang snapped at the towel, while Bill got another grip on her hind flippers and eased her into the wicker chest. The other man closed the box and strapped it tightly shut with the leather lock.

'That wasn't too painful,' Bill smiled, as they hoisted up the box and placed it in the back of the jeep. 'She's a good weight,' said the other man. 'Let's grab a quick cuppa,' said Bill, 'before we head for Dollymount Strand.'

Seafra watched the two nusham walk back to the house. Then she pulled herself over closer to the vehicle. 'Are you all right, Tang?' she asked anxiously.

'Fine, dear Seafra. It's my time to be returned home. I knew it would be soon, but not this soon.'

'You will be fine,' said Seafra.

'I know,' said Tang sadly. 'But I'm going to miss you terribly. You've been such good company.'

'It's I who will miss you,' said Seafra. 'Only for your company I don't think I'd have made it.'

'Listen, Seafra. Your turn will come soon. Prepare yourself. Keep eating and swimming. It will keep you strong and healthy and take your mind off any lonely feelings you may have.'

'I've got them already,' Seafra sighed. She heard a footfall.

The two men walked up the gravelled path. 'Would you look at that!' said the man to Bill pointing at the seal pup. 'She senses what's happening, that we're taking away her companion.' Bill lifted up the seal pup and placed her beside the smaller pool. The dog came over wagging its tail and trying to get into the jeep. 'You stay here,' said Bill to the dog. 'I want you to keep an eye on things while I'm gone. Especially keep an eye on Lady there. She'll be lonely when Tang is gone.' Bill closed the back door and he and the other man got into the vehicle.

Brandy barked loudly as the jeep drove out the gates. Seafra bleated sadly. The dog padded over to the pup and licked her face.

The next few days seemed so long and dreary for Seafra. The bad weather kept the dog and cat indoors. Even the nusham was only seen briefly in the morning and that was to feed Seafra. She didn't feel hungry nor did she want to swim much. Yet she remembered what Tang said about keeping up her strength. She also knew that if she didn't eat, the nusham would force-feed her.

The only pleasure she had was in watching the small birds flitting in and out among the mixed foliage borders. Some, like the little dunnock and blackcap, would skulk about. Others were not as shy and wary. The robin, for example, would venture very close to Seafra, cock its head then fly to a nearby perch. The mistle thrushes and blackbirds spent a great deal of time in a mountain ash feeding on the red berries.

Occasionally Seafra noticed a wren move about in a clump of ivy growing on the shed wall. The malus tree became host to chaffinches and greenfinches. Seafra could see some of the old nests made by them during the breeding season. The berries were what attracted the birds, Seafra realised, as she watched them over the days. Hawthorn, cotoneaster, and the female holly tree all produced an abundance of berries. Seafra knew that the nusham was not only caring for her kind but that he must have planted all these trees and shrubs with the birds and insects in mind.

Creeping honeysuckle, buddleia with its long conical flowers, privet, even sunflowers, poppies, nettles, and thistles, were all visited by wild birds or insects.

Seafra also observed that whereas most of the birds had gone silent this time of year, the robin still sang its melancholy song from a small perch high in an apple tree.

The light began to fade. Seafra decided to settle down for the night. As she made herself comfortable, she scratched, yawned and stretched. Then she noticed her foreflipper had chunks of white fur in the nails. Seafra looked down her body. Large patches of white fur were gone from her belly. She realised she too was changing. Now she could see grey adult fur where the white fluffy fur had been shed.

Her time would soon come, she just had to be patient.

Chapter 8

A dim roseate light permeated the sky. Saoirse had finished swimming and hauled himself out of the water. Lutra and Grypus sat looking out beyond the rocks. Saoirse called to them. They just sat in silence; their thoughts were elsewhere. He moved closer and greeted them again. Saoirse's call brought them back to an awareness of his presence. They turned to him giving him their full attention.

Saoirse felt a chill of apprehension pass over him. 'What's up?' he enquired.

Grypus' nose wrinkled. Then he snorted. 'Dear Saoirse, it's time . . . ' he gave a deep sigh.

'Time for what?' Saoirse asked.

'Listen,' Grypus said. 'Do you hear the soothing sound of the sea? It's calling you!'

'But I'm in the water every day,' Saoirse smiled cheerfully.

'What Grypus means is . . . it's time you departed the island and found your own way. Listen to the waves, look for the signs, they are all there to teach and guide you.'

'But I'm happy here,' said the young seal sadly. 'Why must I leave?'

Grypus looked at him with moist eyes. 'We love your company, but you must look to the sea for your future. It is your true mother; it was the sea that dreamed you and bore you. You are strong and ready now for the great journey through the sea of life. But remember, there's always danger lurking below the surface. Be vigilant.'

'I must be away too,' said Lutra. 'So I will say my farewell and give you my blessing for a long and fulfilled life. I will see you again, dear friend,' he said looking up at Grypus.

'I have no doubt,' the old seal smiled. 'Take good care of yourself and watch out for those discarded nets.'

'I will, don't worry about me,' Lutra retorted.

There was a long silence.

'It's time to rest,' said Grypus.

Saoirse sat listening to the sound of the water well into the depths of the night. He knew his friends were right, he had to make his own way through life. But he began to feel terror at the idea of being alone. Sleep finally overcame him and he slept soundly.

Lutra was gone before the light of dawn touched the sky.

* * *

Saoirse awoke and looked around. Grypus was still asleep by his favourite rock, but Lutra had left. Saoirse turned to face the sea. A deep sadness welled up within him. It would have been nice to travel for a time with Lutra among the jade-green waves. Yet he knew sooner or later they would have to part. Lutra had made the decision for him. Maybe he should stay a few more weeks just to prepare a little better for life alone. A solitary fulmar passed over and floated out to sea on stiff wingbeats.

Saoirse realised the time had come. He would leave that morning. Pulling himself up the bank to tell Grypus of his decision, he stopped and looked at the old seal still sleeping soundly.

I won't disturb him, Saoirse thought. Turning his body he scurried down to the water's edge. Looking back to see if Grypus was stirring, he could hear the loud snoring. He smiled, then with a light touch he eased himself into the water and was away.

Saoirse was feeling a mixture of excitement and dread as he stared out across the limitless water. The perils of the sea began to occupy his mind. What if an orca was watching and waiting for him right now, ready to tear him to pieces? He shuddered at the idea. Then he scolded himself for such thoughts. He'd been out in these waters so many times with Lutra and Grypus and had never seen a killer whale or anything bigger than Grypus.

He turned his head to take a last look at Grypus' island which was moving even further away from him. Heaving a deep sigh he began to feel a loneliness so profound that it hurt, yet he urged himself on. Picking up a steady speed he continued porpoising through the water.

The pleasant thought of returning to the island each evening was now gone. From now on he would have to trust his own instinct. After a time he found his anxiety receding as he pushed onwards. There was only the sound of the waves and his own body cutting through the water. Ahead all he could see was the heaving undulating horizon where the sea and sky met.

Suddenly Saoirse felt a bump to his head, not a hard one, but enough to startle him. He instinctively dived deep under the water to see what had brushed off him. Looking up he could see a strange square shape lying on the skin of the water. Since it hadn't dived down to pursue him, Saoirse decided to investigate. He slowly paddled back to the surface. The object was just a large piece of driftwood. He sniffed at it gingerly. Pushing it with his muzzle a little it felt strong and sturdy. He made several attempts to hoist himself onto it, for it was wider than he was and as long as Grypus.

He finally succeeded in climbing aboard the driftwood. Clumps of seaweed trailed the edges of the wood. There were even a few hitchhikers like barnacles in between the gaps. Saoirse noticed the long hollowed tracks made by ship worms. He poked his snout on a metal object that was bolted to the wood. It still held a faint scent of nusham.

It was quite pleasant taking a rest on the wood and it also gave him a clear view over the waves. He floated gently in the

long swells. The feelings of anxiety were gone as he stared up
at the overcast sky. He was surprised that he wasn't hungry;
normally he awoke ravenous. Looking back there was no sign
of the island. It had completely receded from the horizon.

That was the sad part for Saoirse, to realise the pleasant
return to the island each evening to his friends was now gone.
He lay stretched out on the smooth wood, seeking ease for his
aching limbs. As he settled down his mind ranged over the
events of the past, then switched to the killings. His senses
reeled and he felt both sad and panicky. His body became all
jerky. He turned and lay on his back. If he looked at the sky and
focused on pleasant things perhaps he could banish the black
thoughts.

Moving in strange new waters, Saoirse could see shafts of
sunlight pierce the grey clouds. He settled into a more restful
state. He was now an intrepid explorer he thought, keen to
learn more about life. He lay about in tranquil repose watching
the sun's rays radiate through and send golden shafts down to
the water. The water sloshed over the side of the driftwood; it
was a pleasing sound to his ears. Soon he would succumb to
sleep.

The windless night filled his senses with an eerie silence.
Beyond the sweep of the sea, in the arch of darkness, the stars
twinkled brightly. He tried to identify some of them,
remembering with affection the night Lutra told him about
them. He regretted not having paid more attention at the time;
instead he had taken the chats for granted. He longed for more
conversations like those.

He looked to the heavens and wished, and asked the eternal
ones to guard and protect Lutra and Grypus. Moving quietly
through the darkness he felt as if he was the only one alive in

the vast world of silence.

Dawn brought a beautiful sunrise. The sea was calm. Saoirse was now feeling ravenous. It was time to search for breakfast. He was about to leap off the raft when he heard a strange noise. He listened with bated breath as the sound of a loud exhalation broke the silence. The sound was repeated several times. Each time he heard it, it seemed to be getting closer and closer.

What was it? He became alarmed. Was it some large monster seeing him as a meal? Spray spouted into the sky and a large dark shape was evident just below the surface. There was no place to hide. The creature was heading straight for him.

The raft was rammed, then lifted clean out of the water with Saoirse holding on for dear life. The creature was now carrying Saoirse and the raft through the deep wide swells. Saoirse leaped from the raft into the water and dived down several fathoms. He could see the massive frame of the creature pushing slowly through the water. Then to the young seal's horror the creature began to turn, displacing large masses of water. It was heading for him again. Saoirse had never seen anything like the size of the creature before. It was almost upon him.

Saoirse arched his body violently, propelling himself to the surface, gasping for air. He anticipated the creature's attack any moment. His heart pounded in his chest as he twisted his head from side to side to see where the creature would appear next. It broke the surface several feet away. The head was like a large rock jutting out of the water. The eyes locked on Saoirse. The young seal could do nothing but wait for the creature to make the first move.

'Forgive me for startling you,' said a strong deep voice. 'I was so preoccupied with my thoughts that I didn't notice there was something resting on the driftwood. I hope you aren't hurt?'

It took Saoirse time to find his voice. 'No,' he stammered. 'I'm fine, just . . . just a little shocked to discover there are giant creatures living in the same waters.'

The whale smiled. 'You need have no fear of me,' it said warmly. 'I feed on plankton, not seals.' Its smile broke out into a loud booming laughter.

Saoirse had heard of these tiny organisms called plankton, but wondered how they could satisfy such a large creature. 'You're the biggest fish I've ever seen,' said Saoirse.

'No, I'm not a fish, I'm a whale! A mammal like yourself. A Sei whale to be precise. There are about seventy seven different whale relations. Not all of them live in these waters, of course. Some live in far distant waters.'

'I've heard about those distant waters,' said Saoirse, who was now becoming more relaxed.

'And how did you hear about those far away oceans?' the whale wondered.

'From my friend who is a leathery turtle. His name is Lutra.'

'Lutra . . . ' smiled the whale. 'Is he still going strong? I first met him years ago, when I was young and small like you.'

Saoirse couldn't ever imagine this whale ever being his size.

'Here, climb aboard and you can use me as a raft for a time. I would appreciate the company and we can have a good chat. It shortens the journey.' The whale returned to a horizontal position and Saoirse tried to climb up on its back. It took several attempts as the whale's back was so slippery. Finally he succeeded. 'Let's go,' said the whale.

Saoirse hung on tightly. This was very exciting for him. Much better than the driftwood, he thought. The Sei whale was indeed a gentle giant. Cape was her name, she was heading for the ice kingdom, but was in no hurry, she explained. After questioning Saoirse about his family, she was deeply moved to hear his sad story. Her family too was haunted by the spectre of death. At first she seemed reluctant to talk about it, but as the day wore on she decided to explain what happened to her family and friends.

'On the eve of our departure from the ice kingdom, my mother was most anxious about our long journey west. She claimed she had seen death in the grey clouds. It made the whole herd jumpy, but we couldn't stay around the ice kingdom. Our leader, Marine, had ordered us to get ready to move out.

'There were newly born calves. I was the oldest at the time, having been born the previous season. Most of the young calves had succumbed to shark attacks, drift nets and accidental killing by large passenger vessels bigger than me, that carry the nusham. They travel at great speed through the water.'

Saoirse hadn't seen any of those vessels. He was able to identify the fishing fleets, yachts, the dinghy and the occasional currach. Cape continued and related how after several days at sea the whaling ships came. The nusham were yelling with excitement calling out 'Whales!' It was as if they had a fever and the only way it could be cured was by the sight of red blood on the water.

'We could see the handlebar gun aiming at us. We moved as fast as we could, my parents urging me on. Then a nightmare shape shot from the gunwale. It was a harpoon. It tore into the flesh of one of the elders, then seemed to explode on impact. The herd and the water were in turmoil. Guns were reloaded and they fired again.'

She had seen her mother wince with pain and blood burst from her mouth. Saoirse sensed the tension in Cape's body as she related the story. She moved slowly and silently through the green seas reliving the terrible carnage. After a time she added sadly. 'When the guns stopped roaring then the ropes were turned, reeling in the dead whales.' None but herself survived. 'I watched the factory ship swallow up all my relations one by one. I lay just below the surface paralysed with fear.'

She sighed deeply, then continued. 'My mind was unwilling to accept the horror my eyes had just witnessed. It looked as if the sea itself was bleeding to death. When the factory ship left I can remember the desolate silence that followed. I don't know how I survived the next few weeks. Luckily a pod of dolphins found me and guided me to a different herd of my kind. They adopted me and I stayed with them for several years.'

'Now I'm a bit of a nomad. I'm past the breeding years, but I can say proudly I've raised some strong sons and daughters. I still like to meet with my kin at least once in the year.'

Saoirse began to realise there were few creatures that had not been touched by the nusham reign of terror. They passed near an island of stark cliffs and steep terraces. At the base of one part of the cliff a large blowhole could be seen where water pulsed in and out.

'You must be hungry,' said Cape.

Saoirse responded to the signal to go fishing. He leaped off the whale into the clear blue water. Overhead, gulls wheeled about in a frenzy of excitement. They had spotted something and were swooping greedily on the water. Saoirse kept a safe distance from them, lazily moving in the ebb and flow of a gentle swell. He stared up at the jagged cliffs which plunged sharply to the sea, his eyes narrowing thoughtfully, wondering was he being spied on by the nusham.

There was none to be seen. He dived into the deep and found a large crab that would satisfy him for a time. He could see Cape circling slowly a little further out. Saoirse polished off his meal of crab, then moved away from the cliffs towards his new friend. The gulls were gathering up ahead in large numbers.

Watching them he felt a vague disturbing premonition of death. Perhaps it was because the last time he had seen gulls in such large numbers it was to feed on the dead corpses of his clan. He shuddered at the memory. Perhaps it was only a shoal of fish, he tried to reassure himself.

Cape suddenly surfaced and stared at him. 'It's time we left here,' she said in commanding tones. 'For the safety of the open waters.' Saoirse moved his torpedo-shaped body quickly through the water and hurried out to sea, past a glare path made by the sun, on out through rippling currents. Cape turned her heavy bulk and moved gracefully after him.

The gulls were still screaming and pulling chunks of meat from the surface of the water. Saoirse still could not make out what creature it was. It must be a large one, perhaps like the whale. Then discarded pieces of flesh floated along the water's surface. Saoirse recognised bits of seal fur. He became immobilised with shock when a bloated dead seal brushed off him.

This was what the gulls were feeding on – dead seals. Saoirse remained silent, but his body broke into uncontrollable shivers as he looked at the deep cuts into the skin and blubber. He howled in pain and rage. He so wanted to vent his anger on those nusham who had killed the seals.

Cape nudged him gently. 'Saoirse, this time it's not the nusham.'

The young seal looked puzzled. 'What then?' he snapped and scowled. 'Nusham rubbish? Ropes? Plastics? Nets? Poison? What?'

The whale sensed his frustration and anger. 'I know how you are feeling,' said Cape, 'even though these seals are complete strangers to you. But as I said, it wasn't the nusham.'

'What happened to them then?' Saoirse pleaded. 'Was it orcas?'

The whale turned and moved her head up and down. She seemed to be signalling. A shag flew over and alighted beside them. Saoirse wondered what this little bird knew that he didn't.

'Tell our young friend what you saw,' Cape ordered.

The shag settled some dishevelled feathers on his back. Saoirse waited anxiously. 'They can get very untidy, these feathers, but one must constantly preen and oil them. That's the way they stay in mint condition.'

Cape looked at Saoirse and gave a loud snort. The shag sensed the frustration overcoming the two strangers. He looked at Saoirse then he cleared his throat. 'I first noticed it over a month ago, but I'd had my suspicions . . . you get like that when you've spent a great deal of time at sea, or spying from those steep cliffs, as I have done.' The shag spotted another bloated seal. 'See, there goes another one. You can take my word for it, I know.'

'Know what?' asked Saoirse, not able to conceal his frustration.

'That every wave . . . ' the shag continued, 'seems to pulse with hidden dangers.'

'Speak plainly.' The whale raised the shag and Saoirse clear out of the water.

The shag opened his wings and began to dry them. 'Better than a rock,' he smiled, indicating the mighty form of the whale. Saoirse looked aghast as, peering around, he could see the scattered corpses of seals floating on the surface. The gulls sat on the cliff, bloated from all their gorging. 'I'm never surprised what happens out there,' the shag indicated towards the sea.

Saoirse nudged the shag and stuck his whiskered face up to the shag's red eye. 'Tell me what you know. Now!'

'Take it easy,' said the shag, 'I'm getting to it.' The shag stretched its neck, then settled it back into a resting position. 'One night during the last full moon, I noticed strange forms swimming out from the darkness.'

'What strange forms?' asked the young seal.

'I didn't know what they were at the time . . . they looked a bit like your whale friend, but I realised quickly it was not a solitary creature . . . more like a pack . . . ' He broke off from what he was relating and turning to Saoirse began to tremble. 'You are in unspeakable danger,' he warned. 'Get away from here now, before it's too late.'

Saoirse gave a deep sigh. 'What are you talking about? Nusham? Orcas? What?'

The shag leaped from the whale, descended into the water and began to move away.

'The black hordes,' he called over his shoulder.

Saoirse dived into the water and swam after the shag. 'For the last time make yourself clear. What are the black hordes?'

'Have you not eyes, can you not see?' said the shag. 'If these seals were not killed by the nusham or killer whales, what other creature could inflict such damage?'

'I don't know,' Saoirse insisted.

The shag took flight. As soon as it was airborne and freed of the water it turned its head and squealed: 'Seals!'

Saoirse could not believe what he was hearing. The idea that seals would turn cannibal was inconceivable. Saoirse paused, looking out at the great expanse of the sea, quiet and restful in the soft evening light. 'There must be some other explanation,' he pleaded.

Cape looked at him intently. 'Perhaps,' she answered doubtfully. 'Saoirse, young friend, why don't you come with me and visit the ice kingdom?'

Saoirse was grateful for the invitation but declined the offer. He would love to travel and see the far off seas and the ice kingdom, but something inside him told him he must stay and search out his own destiny beside the waters where he was born. Besides, there were so many questions which he felt could only be answered if he stayed.

Cape knew what he had decided and said her farewell. Then she turned her great bulk and moved away through the water with a graceful but powerful motion.

Saoirse stared over the waves and watched the whale's fluke wave farewell, then disappear below the surface. He sat upright in the water wondering where these black hordes might be lurking.

A cold wind blew across the sea causing him to shiver. Tonight he would sleep on the big island.

Chapter 9

Seafra's family had travelled great distances in search of their lost child. Seafra's mother, Marel, was convinced she was still alive. Kaj, her father, was not so sure. His other wives were prepared to continue the search for Marel's sake. They had questioned a basking shark but he had seen nothing of the young pup. Razorbills, guillemots, puffins, shearwaters, gulls, even choughs, were all asked had they sighted an orphaned white puppy. The answer was always the same. They had not seen her.

They spoke to other colonies of greys and commons. They too had lost young pups during the breeding season. They could sympathise with Marel but were unable to help. Some seals told of the recent terrible massacre on the west coast, where the rookery was completely wiped out by the dreaded nusham. After accepting food and shelter they rested for a time, then continued their search – seal haunts, remote coastal areas, sheltered waters, sandbanks – anywhere a young seal might take refuge. They did not find Seafra.

'It's time we returned home,' Kaj declared.

Marel knew her husband was right. They had searched and searched without any success. She knew she would probably bear more offspring in the future, but Seafra was her first born. If only she could be sure that Seafra survived the storm and was alive somewhere, that would ease the pain of the loss. Most of the time Marel was haunted with images of Seafra dying of hunger and neglect, which produced a deadly melancholy within her.

The eleven seals began their long journey back to Raven's

Point, porpoising together in slow steady rhythm. Up ahead Marel noticed the protruding shape of a common gull as it lazed about between short crested waves. She hurried past her husband and the others. 'I will just ask one more creature.'

The gull saw the grey seal hurrying towards him and he was about to take flight when Marel called out. 'Wait!' The common gull settled back into a relaxed position. Marel drew closer until she was whisker close to the gull. 'Have you seen a young seal puppy?'

'Well, I've seen a great number of them over the years,' the gull replied.

'Recently, I mean,' said Marel. 'She had a white coat, well, it would of course be moulted by now . . .'

The rest of the seals circled the gull. It became a little anxious.

'It's all right, never fear,' said Kaj.

'What was the pup's name?' the gull asked.

'Seafra,' said Marel sadly.

'Seafra! Seafra!' the common gull repeated as if trying to recall where he had heard the name. Then he said brightly. 'I remember a beautiful young grey seal called Seafra!'

'You do?' Marel asked excitedly. 'Is she safe? Where is she?'

The male seal looked on a little suspiciously at the gull. 'I did see her,' insisted the gull. 'She is safe, but is not to be found around these parts. I have never spoken with her, but I knew a friend of hers. Her name was Tang, she . . . '

'Has she returned home?' Marel asked, unable to control her excitement.

The gull went silent.

'What is it? We need to know,' snapped Kaj.

'She is living in the home of a nusham.'

The seals couldn't believe what they were hearing. 'Is this some kind of joke?' growled Kaj. 'If it is, it's in extremely poor taste.'

'It's true,' said the gull. 'I swear by the great spirit that made us all.'

'Oh no,' said Marel. 'Our poor child will be killed like all the others on the west coast.'

'No,' said the gull. 'This nusham is a kind soul.'

'How can you tell?' asked one of the other seals.

'Because the same nusham repaired my injured wing. He cares for common and grey seals. Even an otter and fox have been cared for by him until they were well again.'

'Then what happens?' Marel asked.

'The nusham brings them back to where he first found them.'

'It's hard to believe,' said the seals among themselves.

'Our experience of nusham has always spelt trouble,' Kaj grumbled.

'I've gone back to visit the sanctuary several times. I should know!' the gull insisted.

Marel was greatly relieved to know young Seafra was safe and to think some day she would be returned to the freedom of the sea. They thanked the gull for giving them such wonderful news.

'Glad to be of service,' he said, and flew away.

Now they could journey home, sure in the knowledge that Seafra had survived the storm and was being well taken care of, even if it was by a nusham. They began their long voyage back to Raven's Point.

Kaj was so pleased that his young daughter had survived her frightening ordeal, and he was doubly joyful to see Marel's spirits lifted. He watched her sleek, graceful movement ahead of him. The terrible anxiety was gone. There was a sense of joy from her that he could almost feel through the waves.

On and on they pushed through the banking seas. Kaj looked to the sky, watching the dark scuds of clouds pass over. The weather was beginning to deteriorate. Up ahead, Marel noticed a flock of scoters disperse from where they were dozing on the surface. They lifted from the water with great urgency. She became tense, hoping it wasn't an orca. Perhaps it was a shoal of fish. Maybe the ducks had spotted them. She watched them descend and return to the water a good distance away.

Kaj caught up with her, causing her to start as he brushed along her flank. 'You seem jumpy,' he nuzzled her gently.

She smiled warmly back. 'It's just when one is in alien waters one becomes more wary.'

There was a loud crack of thunder which startled the herd. 'We're all becoming jumpy like young puppies,' Kaj laughed heartily. 'Anyone would think we never heard the sound of thunder before.' They smiled and relaxed. 'I don't know about the rest of you, but I'm ravenous. It's time we had our breakfast. Must keep up our strength, you know.'

'You don't need any excuses,' said one of the other seals. This brought loud laughter from Kaj.

'Don't worry, dear. I'll catch you a nice juicy conger eel,' said another.

'Make sure it's a big one,' said Marel, patting her big stomach with her foreflipper.

Marel felt a sudden chill of apprehension but couldn't understand why. The wind began to pick up. The sky seemed to empty and the rain beat down in heavy sheets. Soon the sea was like a cauldron, the waves boiling and crashing down. The seals were tossed about, submerging, then bobbing up again.

'We'll have to wait until this storm blows over before we get that well-earned breakfast,' Kaj bellowed.

The winds continued to churn up the water as they rolled and spun about. They were pulverised by the waves for most of the morning until the storm finally blew itself out. As the sky began to clear they watched an arrowhead of birds pass over. Marel was relieved to be free of the storm's grip. Her body was an aching vessel from all the knocking about, although she was used to these sudden storms. Normally she would have the sense to climb ashore and let it blow out, but there was no sign of land nearby to take refuge.

Still, all was calm again. She sighed with relief. She circled about, scanning the distant waters. All seemed calm, but then she noticed ripples again. It was as if the waves were turning black. How curious, she thought. She nudged Kaj who was 'bottling' after the storm.

'What is it?' he blurted. 'I was just grabbing forty winks,' he said, excusing himself.

'Look!' she indicated the dark pattern just below the surface. It was like some strange creature in a deadly hunt. The seals became fascinated by the movement. At first, black ridges could be seen just above the water, then the pattern changed, forming a wide circle that enclosed them.

'It's seals,' said Kaj with a sigh of relief. He hoped they were friendly. If they weren't he would give them as good as they gave. At worst they might end up with a few bites or scrapes. Kaj knew that when he explained why they were here and assured them they were not trying to move into anyone's territory, everything would be fine.

Kaj and his family grouped together back to back. There was a deadly silence as they waited for the other seals to show themselves. A cold fear wrapped itself around Marel as she waited in dreaded anticipation.

Suddenly they were all around them, each one breaking the surface at the same time. Kaj and his family stared aghast upon the black seals. They had never seen such hideous creatures before, with red bulging eyes and gaunt faces, white and green lesions on their black-skinned bodies. Kaj stammered out a greeting to them.

One black seal, who seemed to be the leader, just gave them a cold, cruel stare that seemed to bore into them.

'What happened to you?' Marel enquired sympathetically.

The leader grinned and flashed his sharp teeth, then a loud scream issued from him which seared through the air. Suddenly the black seals lunged through the water towards Kaj. They hissed and spat as they attacked him. The combined weight of the black seals crushed Kaj as they bore down on him. He gasped for air as he tried valiantly to defend his family. Soon his blood stained the water.

Marel felt the blacks move around and beneath her. Their eyes bulged with the message of murder. Marel fought with all her strength, snapping and pushing at her assailants. As they fought, the green and red water was boiling and seething. She could feel the sharp bites to her back and neck as they swirled about her. She cried to her sisters but they were not faring any better.

Marel was forced down towards the sea bed and felt as if her chest was about to split open. Darkness was closing in on her. Her lungs ached as her body seemed to lose all feeling. As the fierce wave of seals continued to attack she kicked and tried to free herself from the writhing bodies that hung on like parasites. A voice sounded in her head. It was the leader yelling: 'Leave none of them alive.'

With a last desperate effort she managed to free herself and hurry towards the surface. Flippers flailed wildly as her head broke the surface. A mass of movement below her moved in for the kill. She drew in large gulps of air, panting hard. The crimson water touched her foreflipper as she stared sadly at one of her sisters, lying still on the surface, oozing blood.

Something began to pull at her hind flippers. In a few seconds she disappeared below the surface having gasped her final breath.

Chapter 10

Justine and Deirdre had been awake since six o'clock. As Mary stepped out of the shower and began to dry herself she could hear them jumping on their beds. She checked her watch. Seven o'clock. Why did she stay up so late chatting, she scolded herself. As she left the bathroom Chappie passed her.

'Good morning, did you sleep well?' she enquired.

'Like a log, thank the good Lord.'

A thump sounded through the ceiling. 'Will you girls stop that racket and come down for breakfast,' she yelled loudly.

'How can two little girls sound so like a herd of charging wildebeest!' Chappie sniggered

Mary smiled. 'Would you like a nice fry-up?' she asked.

Chappie beamed back. 'Have I ever refused such a delicious offer?'

'Maybe I shouldn't be encouraging you to eat all those rashers, sausages and puddings.'

'Ah sure something will have to get me in the end,' he retorted. 'Did you ever sit in one of those restaurants and the customer is dictating to the poor waitress. No white toast, only brown, one egg, soft! No butter, only sunflower oil! De-caffeinated coffee. Sure they might as well go and live in a Tibetan monastery up in the Himalayas. Anyone can see they're stressed out and they think sunflower or soya spread is going to help. It's important to be able to enjoy yourself. Otherwise sure you're not living at all, only existing.'

'Well, don't worry, you'll get your full Irish breakfast, white bread and butter included.'

He laughed and followed her down the stairs. 'Today is the big day, then,' he yelled after her as she went into the kitchen.

'Yes . . . sure the girls have been awake since six,' she replied.

As they sat having breakfast Justine asked what time would they be bringing back the seal.

'I told you . . . around midday.'

'I forgot,' said Justine.

'No, you didn't,' Deirdre retorted. 'You said it to me upstairs.'

'Sure it's very exciting,' said Chappie, shovelling a piece of egg and sausage into his mouth. 'I wonder will we recognise the little seal, probably all grown up,' he added.

'Well, they're expecting a big turnout,' said Mary. 'The local papers will be there. South East Radio is going to make a programme on it. The national papers are going to send photographers.'

'So they should, isn't it a good story for a change. Most of the time it's horror stories . . . Media poisoning, that's what it is.'

'Don't upset yourself,' said Mary. 'We don't want you falling off that hobby-horse of yours.'

Chappie grumbled to himself, then brightened up by producing four rolls of film for the camera. 'We'll get it all on record, the seal release.'

'Deadly!' said Justine.

'Wrap yourselves up well,' said Mary. 'It's lovely and bright now but the weather forecast is for a cold, windy day.'

They arrived at the beach at eleven thirty. Hundreds of people were gathered in the car park at Curracloe. Bunting hung around The Winning Post. Everyone was getting free tea, coffee and sandwiches from the owner and his family.

Music filled the air as traditional players performed on

fiddles, banjos and bodhrans. Justine and Deirdre could see all their school friends running up and down the sand dunes. They hurried over to join them. There was a wonderful festival atmosphere. Politicians, local county councillors, Gardai, even people from the diving clubs were all there looking forward to the seal release.

'Isn't it wonderful to see such a turnout, to celebrate a young seal's return to the wild,' said Mary.

'It does your heart good,' said Chappie, wiping a moist eye with his handkerchief.

There were loud cheers as the young seal arrived. Bill Fortune was amazed at the number of people who had turned out for the event. He was greeted by the warden and the wildlife ranger. They helped him lift the wicker chest from the back of the jeep.

The crowds hurried over. A large circle of spectators formed around Bill. Then he lifted up the lid to reveal the young seal. Cameras clicked and camcorders recorded the event. Then he put the seal into a holding pen so that children and adults could get a good view.

Bill Fortune had a cup of coffee put in his right hand while a reporter pushed a microphone towards him. He was questioned about the conflict between fishermen and seals. His head was soon in a spin from all the questions about depleting fish stocks, and seals taking fishermen's livelihood away from them.

Mary could see he was in a bit of a spot so she pushed through the crowd of reporters and linked him over to the platform, where he and the Minister for the Environment got a chance to say a few words and to thank everyone for turning up and making the day such a special occasion. There were loud cheers and applause.

Seafra was carried down to the beach in the wicker chest by four strong men. The crowds were asked to make a wide wall on either side of the chest. The divers at this stage had entered the water to make sure the seal didn't get into any difficulties. The warden and ranger warned that seals bite, so they asked people not to try and pet it.

All of the children were requested to link hands to hold the adults back. This brought loud laughter. The children were only too willing to be of service. Justine and Deirdre were to officially release the seal back to the sea. With Bill's help the wicker chest was tilted and the young seal crawled out. It gave a small bark. Everyone cheered as they watched it move along the sand towards the sea. The children were squealing and moved closer.

All attention was riveted on the seal and the two young girls who were the first to follow behind her. Chappie squeezed through the crowds to take some photographs. The girls smiled. The seal turned back once and all the children screamed with excitement and laughter.

Seafra got the smell of the sea in her nostrils and it felt so good. She turned and made her way towards the sea again. This brought more loud cheers. She propelled herself forward; she would be glad when she got away from all these nusham. Though for some reason she wasn't as frightened as she had been when she first saw them.

She would like to have said 'thanks' to the nusham who looked after her, but how does one communicate with a nusham. She had no idea. Her foreflippers touched the shoreline and a wave washed over them. In a moment she would be back where she belonged, in the sea.

She raised her head and looked back once at the two young nusham immediately behind her. Then she was away. There were loud cheers from the crowds. Seafra began to porpoise. It felt wonderful to be back in the water. Turning on her back she scratched and stretched. The nusham in the water watched from a distance. From now on the sea would be her mother and provide for her.

Mary got a last glimpse of the silver grey body as the seal hurried out to sea.

'Will she be all right?' Justine asked her mother.

'She'll be fine. She's strong and healthy.'

Chappie moved up through the crowds. 'My feet are soaking,' he grumbled. 'A sneaky wave washed over them when I was trying to get that last picture.'

'You're worse than these two,' Mary jeered, pointing to the girls.

'Well, it was worth it; I think I've got an excellent shot of her just about to take the plunge.'

'Look,' said Deirdre, pointing to the scruff marks made by the seal. 'That's all that's left,' she sighed.

'Come and join us for lunch, Bill,' said Mary.

'No,' said Chappie. 'You are all joining me for lunch in Wexford town. Now, you can't refuse an offer like that,' he insisted.

'You're on,' said Bill. 'Come in the jeep.'

Mary climbed in the passenger side. Chappie, the warden, the ranger, and the two girls climbed in the back.

'Phew,' said Justine. 'There's a terrible smell.'

'That's from the seal,' said Bill. 'I've had to put up with that all the way from Dublin.'

They all laughed loudly.

Chapter 11

Saoirse sat on a large, sharp and jagged rock and watched the white surf curling onto the sheltered waters. He felt the warmth of the morning sun on his face. The bouts of nausea, which had been brought on by witnessing the destruction of the seals, were gone. He began to feel relaxed and calm again. As he lay staring into the jade waves of the Atlantic he began to be lulled to sleep.

The harsh call of a peregrine startled him as she lifted from a cushion of campions and wheeled into the sky. He could see the culprit that had disturbed the falcon; it was a great black-backed gull combing the cliffs in search of eggs or young chicks. As Saoirse turned his head to settle back into a restful position he became aware of movement out at sea, beyond where the seaweed was swirling in the tide.

Large black forms stole across the water's surface. Waves parted as tall black fins tore the surface. Some of the fins were taller than others. Saoirse had never seen killer whales before but he knew instinctively that they were the creatures Grypus and Lutra had warned him about. He watched as the whales spouted and gulped air. Water vapours made small rainbows in the air. There was a sonorous noise as they shadowed below the surface.

It was a pod of twenty orcas. He knew their very presence was an overture to death and was certainly grateful he hadn't been caught out in the bay with those. He listened to their fast clicking noises as they moved out to sea and felt very sorry for any unfortunate seals that might cross their path. They moved at deadly speed out through the surging waters.

Saoirse stayed put until late afternoon to make sure the orcas were gone. Then he made his way carefully out into the tide. He kept close to the large island as he was still a bit jumpy after seeing the killer whales. Kittiwakes, guillemots, razorbills, shags and puffins continued their noisy business above on the cliffs, each busy feeding young or incubating eggs. They had no real fear of the orcas, they were more concerned with the gulls and skuas which were a constant threat during the breeding season.

A shadow passed over Saoirse. He looked up to see a gannet flying high overhead, inspecting a wider area of water so it could dive headlong into the sea after a mackerel. Around the next inlet things were quieter. He did a little fishing himself. After catching three fish in quick succession he felt good and full, so he rolled and splashed and frolicked about in the currents.

There was a sudden distant noise. Sound travels so quickly underwater that he instantly became aware of it. Peering over the waves he could see a small fishing boat in the distance. It seemed to be steering a course towards him. Wherever there was a boat, there were nusham. Any sign of nusham made him very anxious. It was time to get away; he hoped the killer whales were long gone.

As he began to swim off he noticed small circular objects bobbing in the water. He had seen them before but had never been this close to them. Some were brightly coloured, pink, blue and white. They seemed to be attached to something for they were not washed away by the tides. A voice inside seemed to be telling him to go and investigate them. He checked the progress of the boat; it appeared stationary. So swimming over to the ball-shaped object he sniffed at it.

The scent of nusham which he detested was very strong from it. He could hear the engine starting up, the boat was coming closer. The engine went silent again. Saoirse followed the rope down to the sea bed. There he could see the lobster pot where crabs and lobsters had found their way in, to get the tasty morsel of fish that was used to bait the creatures. Once they were inside they scrambled over each other to find an escape route without any success. Saoirse felt sorry for them but there was nothing he could do.

He could see several ropes placed at different spots and the deadly traps for lobsters attached to them. One of the distant ropes seemed to be more slack than the other ones. Saoirse noticed that there was something floating beside the rope, a few feet below the buoy. The shape looked familiar but the water was murky and visibility was poor. He decided to take a closer look.

The engine started up again. He watched the boat making a semi-circle. It was now behind him. He could see its black shape above on the surface. Then he saw the rope being pulled and the lobster pot was hauled up. He hurried over to the distant lobster pot. As he drew closer he recoiled in horror. Hanging from the rope was his dear friend Lutra, his limp body motionless.

Saoirse circled the turtle and could see that his left flipper was tangled in the rope.

'Lutra! Lutra!' Saoirse cried. As he nosed the turtle's head the eyes were closed, then one eye opened to a slit.

'Saoirse?' said the turtle weakly. 'How good to see you again . . .'

'What happened?' Saoirse asked sadly.

'I don't really know. One minute I was avoiding a discarded net left by the nusham, next minute I swam straight into this rope. I guess I must have panicked and ended up entangling myself.'

The engine started up again and the boat was heading straight for them.

'Save yourself, dear boy,' said the turtle. 'There's no point in us both being destroyed.'

'No,' said Saoirse. 'I will not leave you.'

'Please,' said Lutra mustering all his strength. 'I order you!'

'You saved me once, when I was a helpless puppy. I'll never forget that.'

'I've lived a long and full life. You have all your life ahead of you.'

'Save your strength,' Saoirse pleaded.

Saoirse could see the other lobster pots being pulled out of the water. This one would be next. The nusham would not spare the old turtle; they might even have the death guns with them. The water was being churned up as the engine started again. Saoirse had to think rapidly; his friend was fading fast and the fishing boat was almost upon them.

Then he noticed the net Lutra had mentioned. Saoirse propelled himself down and pulled at the net. It would not budge. He pulled again and again, the plastic cord cutting the side of his mouth. He began to panic as he pulled with all his might. The boat was now a few feet away from the rope which had ensnared Lutra.

He would try just once more. Pulling and growling, he stretched his body fully back. Then he heard a rock tumble and the net became undone. He quickly swam up to the boat, to where the outboard motor was churning the water. He was terrified of the noise and the sharp blades but he had to get as close as possible to be sure the blades would become entangled and hopefully stop the boat. Swimming a few inches below the blades with the net trailing above him, it touched the blades and there was such a jerk it nearly choked him. He quickly let go of the net. A grinding noise and a snapping sound followed before the engine stopped.

He could hear the nusham cursing as they peered over the edge.

'I think we hit a seal,' yelled one man.

'No, there it goes.' They watched Saoirse dive to the bottom.

'We hit something,' growled an other man. 'The motor won't start.'

They began to hoist it out of the water. 'Oh bloody hell! What fool threw that net away.' He pulled out his pen-knife and began to cut the netting from the propeller.

This gave Saoirse enough time to hurry back to Lutra and assess the situation. He saw where the rope had bitten into the skin of the turtle. He would have to try and chew through the rope; it was the only way. Lutra at this stage had lost consciousness and was floating spread-eagled like a creature already dead.

'You can't die,' Saoirse pleaded. Then he began to chew on the rope with all the savagery he could manage. His jaws and lips ached. He felt his mouth fill with his own blood.

'That's cleared that,' said the man with the knife. 'I thought we were going to be stuck here all day.'

'You're a topper,' said the other man. 'I'd like to get my hands on the idiot who dumped the net over the side.'

'Happens all the time,' said the first man as he started up the engine. It caught first time and they sped over to the lobster pot where Lutra and Saoirse were.

Saoirse let go of the rope momentarily from fright.

'Let's get this one up,' said one of the men.

Saoirse could see he had almost gnawed through the rope.

'One more to change!'

He clamped his jaws over the chewed section. At last, the rope was bitten in two. The turtle floated down to the deep.

The man pulled and a small portion of rope came to the surface. He examined it and saw it had been chewed through. 'What the hell!' he exclaimed. 'What did this?'

'Maybe one of those blue sharks,' said the other man.

'More likely that seal that was snooping about here. Probably after an easy meal. Damn it! I've lost a new lobster pot over it.'

Lutra lay on the seabed, the rope still attached to his flipper. Saoirse would now have to bite through another section to free him from the lobster pot. His friend needed help quickly if he was not to perish. Saoirse worked on chewing the rope again. His left forepaw held one part down as he chewed and chewed on the rope. Soon he had bitten it clean through.

The boat began to move away. Saoirse hoisted the old turtle onto his back. He gently took the twisted rope from the turtle's front flipper. The cuts were deep, blood freely oozed from the wounds. Saoirse swam to the surface and gulped the fresh air then went back down to get the turtle. He adjusted Lutra to get him into a comfortable position on his back. He was glad it wasn't on land. There would be no way he could have managed to carry him.

He wedged the turtle's good flipper under his right foreflipper and eased his way up to the surface. The weather was fine; there was a light breeze producing short crested waves which suited Saoirse fine.

There was only one place to take poor Lutra where he would be safe, that was to Grypus' island. It would be great to be back on the island with the two of them; it would be just like old times. In fact, it was only several months since he'd left the island, yet it seemed a lifetime ago.

If he could just avoid the killer whales and the black seals, things would be fine. He hadn't seen any sight of them, but had seen their ferocious attacks on that unfortunate group of seals they happened upon. He kept alert to any sound or movement but the only sound was the sea and his body moving through the water. The occasional auk or gull would come into his line of vision but they were of no concern to him. A pod of dolphin were frolicking in the distance. Again, he knew they would not bother him.

As they penetrated deeper into the sea, he began to ponder where the black seals had come from and why they had become cannibals. What catastrophe had befallen them? Saoirse had heard about the distemper virus, of viral pneumonia, pleurisy, and other diseases that affected his kind, but this was something very different.

He recalled one evening when Grypus had told him about an

outbreak of deadly disease that killed nearly two thousand common seals and about three hundred of their kind; it had happened when his mother was a pup.

The faint voice of the old turtle sounded in his ear. 'Where am I?' said Lutra weakly.

Saoirse was overjoyed to hear Lutra speak. He was beginning to fear the worst as he hadn't heard anything from Lutra for several hours.

'You're safe!' Saoirse said warmly. 'There's a quiet cove where we can rest up for the night. We should be there before starlight.' The young seal surged on, more determined than ever to get Lutra to a safe haven for the night. A northerly wind began to blow cold. Waves washed over the back of Lutra. Saoirse pushed onwards, occasionally being tossed about in the tumbling sea.

The stinging spray began to hurt his eyes as he was buffeted by the rough seas. They were now being rolled and pitched in the heavy swells. It was difficult to keep the large-framed turtle from sliding off his back in these conditions. Then to his great joy he saw the cove where they could find shelter.

Heavy clouds passed overhead. Soon they'd be caught up in the pounding waves that would hit the island. With a burst of energy Saoirse pierced through the waves, until another larger one lifted them up and threw them with full force onto the sandy shore. They had become separated and the two of them lay exhausted on the washline. Lutra began to struggle anxiously, for the waves had thrown him down on his back. He could not turn himself. He called to Saoirse for help but there was no answer. The young seal had been knocked out by the waves that had deposited him on the shore.

Five great black-backed gulls circled overhead, followed by two ravens. They alighted on the rocks to assess the situation.

The turtle looked like it was in the last throes of life. The seal seemed lifeless. They hopped down on the sand and cautiously moved over to their potential meals.

A wheatear was scurrying about, ever alert and searching for sand hoppers. It stepped on to Saoirse's hind flippers and searched between the digits on his slippery webbed flippers. Saoirse felt a tickling sensation and shifted his hind flipper. The wheatear flew away and landed behind a clump of bird's-foot trefoil.

A great black-backed gull hammered down on Saoirse's head. The young seal gave out a loud yelp which startled the gulls and ravens. With a clatter of wings they lifted from the shore and flew out to sea in different directions. Saoirse raised his head; he was feeling rather dizzy and had double vision momentarily. As he turned his neck he saw poor Lutra in the spread-eagled position lying on his carapace.

He hurried over to him. Using his muzzle, he pushed with his whole body and successfully flipped the turtle over until it was in its proper position.

Lutra gave a sigh of relief. 'I can breathe properly again,' he said and coughed loudly.

After resting up for some time, Saoirse decided they both needed some food. 'Will you be all right on your own?' he asked. The turtle blinked back and nodded he would. Saoirse eased himself into the water. Soon he was completely submerged. Hunger gave him an edge; he was very focused in pursuit of prey. It wasn't long till he had caught a cod and a crab. It took a great deal of searching for him to find Lutra's delicacy, and then he picked up several small moon jellyfish.

Lutra watched as Saoirse came surging out of the waves and hauled himself up the sandy cove. The water broke over him several times before he reached a dry spot. His mouth was full of jellyfish which he placed in front of the old turtle.

'The sight of these is bringing my appetite back,' Lutra said warmly.

'When did you last eat?' the young seal enquired.

'Weeks ago,' said the old turtle.

'Weeks!' said Saoirse in amazement.

'Oh, I have gone without food for months at a stretch,' said Lutra casually.

'I must eat every day,' said Saoirse, 'or I'd be starving with the hunger.' As he watched the turtle chomping into the jellyfish he asked how he could possibly eat them.

'They're delicious, you should try them,' Lutra retorted.

'No thanks, I'll stick to meaty fish.'

'Have you eaten?' asked Lutra.

'Yes, I had a delicious cod and a shore crab,' Saoirse mimicked his old friend.

The turtle burped with satisfaction. 'I'm quite full.'

'How is your flipper?' asked Saoirse.

The turtle had almost forgotten his injury. 'With some good food and rest I should be on the mend in a few weeks.'

The night began to creep in. A break in the clouds helped them to catch a glimpse of the stars. Saoirse was reminded of that special night when he was a pup and Lutra and Grypus explained the mystery of the lights in the sky.

Saoirse's thoughts darkened as he explained to Lutra about the black seals that preyed on other seals. Lutra did not appear surprised, but Saoirse could see he was disturbed as he related the events of the day when he and Cape, the Sei whale, had come across the bloated and torn bodies of the dead seals.

Lutra sat for a long time in silence looking out at the crested waves and hearing the crash and hiss of the surf. Then he explained how he heard at a cormorant colony that the nusham had been experimenting with strange chemicals and had captured a large group of seals.

'The story goes that the nusham injected the seals with some deadly nuclear chemicals to test their levels of resistance. The result was it drove some of the seals crazy, and caused physical malformation in others. The plan was then to destroy the seals. But for some unknown reason the seals escaped and have been roaming the seas ever since. I heard that story over four summers ago, but thankfully I've never seen them. Many species have told me about them, or have heard stories. They became known as the black phantoms of the seas. But it's quite alarming to think they might be in these waters.'

Then on a brighter note, he was delighted to hear Saoirse had met his old friend Cape and that she was alive and well. The moon appeared as the clouds dispersed. Lutra lay his weary head down on the soft sand. 'Will you excuse me, dear boy, but I can barely keep my eyes open.' He gave a big yawn, closed his eyes and was asleep in an instant.

Saoirse smiled a contented smile, knowing his dear friend had come back from the edge of life again. Tomorrow he would be with Grypus and Lutra on the island again. This pleased him greatly. Saoirse laid his head down and tried to settle into sleep. He just lay there listening to the sound of the sea and the wind, but sleep would not come. He gazed out across the silvery light and listened to the manx shearwaters calling in the distance.

Then his sharp eyes noticed something move in the silver-tipped waves. It was a lone seal moving slowly through the water like a shadow. Was it one of the black seals spying on them? Were they waiting in ambush? Saoirse scanned the waters but could see no others. He watched for a time. The seal seemed to be simply enjoying itself in the water. Maybe it was a stranger to these parts, unaware of the dangers that lay in the dark waters, of the black seals and pack of orcas that were probably prowling below the surface at this very moment.

Saoirse felt he should warn the stranger and offer it shelter in the cove. The seal was now wallowing in some nearby seaweed. Saoirse plopped into the water and ventured over. The streamlined shape of the stranger had moved from the seaweed and was heading out to sea again, body gleaming in the moonlight as it porpoised out into the deep.

Then the stranger stopped and pulled itself to attention as it spotted Saoirse chasing and slapping the surface of the water. Saoirse did not want to startle the stranger by sneaking up on it. He hoped his sounds and movement would be interpreted as friendly as he approached the ghostly outline of the seal.

The stranger extended its neck and gave out a growl. Saoirse gathered his courage and moved closer. He circled and bobbed up and down. Now he was only a few feet away. His eyes opened wide as he looked upon her. She was the most beautiful creature he had ever encountered. He moved beside her, enthralled at the magic of her presence. She blinked warmly back at him, the moonlight reflected in her eyes. They sniffed each other in recognition, then slowly circled each other as if in a dance of destiny. Saoirse felt as if he was enveloped in a beautiful dream. They stopped, locked in each other's gaze.

'What is your name?' Saoirse asked. His body trembled.

'Seafra,' she said tenderly.

He felt the shock of love that only comes to the young, as they waded in the magical light, her eyes warming him with a gentle tenderness. She smiled and said coquettishly. 'You make your love as visible as the moon.'

Saoirse looked embarrassed, then she licked his face and gently brushed off him. All fears and anxieties melted away in her presence. They stayed in the water frolicking and playing. Then he invited her to stay at the cove with him and his friend, Lutra. Seafra was so pleased with such special company that she accepted the offer. The two swam silently back to shore.

They talked all night under the silvery moon. Seafra heard the tragic story about his family and how he came to meet Lutra and Grypus. Seafra then related what had happened to her and how she had been cared for by a kind nusham. Saoirse could hardly believe it, that there were any kind and caring nusham; he thought they were all born enemies of wildfolk. Then Seafra told the sad story about her family. How she had returned to Raven's Point to be told they had all left in pursuit of her. Her eyes moistened over. 'Then a common gull I met told me that they had been brutally killed by the black seals, a savage horde of vicious killers that roam the seas.'

'I'm aware of them,' said Saoirse, heaving a deep sigh. His own personal tragedy seemed to pale when he heard her story. After a long silence he asked what she was going to do. She said she would follow the tides and currents and allow life to happen, to unfold in its own way.

'Well, this is why we must have met,' said Saoirse excitedly. 'It must be fate. Two stars meeting in the night sky.'

'Colliding,' she smiled as she tried to stifle a yawn.

'You must be tired,' he said anxiously.

'A little!' she answered softly. Then she lay down on the cold soft sand. Lutra, listening to all the love talk, chuckled quietly to himself as the two seals lay down to sleep.

* * *

Dawn had crept over the eastern sky. The stars began to fade in the grey light. Then the orange disc sun was revealed in the silent light. Saoirse shivered and awoke. He raised his head, blinking at the low shafts of sunlight. He had not slept long but felt completely refreshed. He had dreams of golden seas where he swam and frolicked with his beloved Seafra. It was an exquisite dream; he wished he could still continue it. Yet the vision of his dreams was alongside him sleeping soundly. He just stared, watching her beautiful form. He hoped her dreams were as beautiful.

He listened to her gentle breathing. He remembered their encounter the previous night among the silvery waves and he ached with love. He so wanted to call out to the waves and tell them to carry his feeling to all the sea creatures. He heard Lutra snoring and shifting. Saoirse decided he would slip into the water and catch breakfast for the three of them. The morning was cold but bright. The shock of the chilly waters brushed any sleepiness from his body.

He propelled himself through the waves which seemed a lot calmer than yesterday. What should he bring her to eat, he wondered. If he could catch a salmon, he was sure she would love it. Lutra should be able to handle a big crab. He had seen him eating them before. Yes, he would catch a large salmon for his love that they could share . . . from now on he would share his life with her, he decided. That is, if she agreed and wanted to.

He thought anxiously. He hoped she would. Well, he would take things as they came, he told himself, and not try to force the situation. Nobody told him before that such a love could exist and hit one like a bolt of lightning from the blue. Of course he knew about love before, the special love for his parents, his family, then a different love for Lutra and Grypus, Cape the Sei whale; there seemed to be so many types of love.

But the feeling he felt for Seafra was overwhelming; it was cosmic, as Lutra would say when speaking of some great event. While Saoirse was away with his own thoughts and feelings he was totally unaware of movement below the surface. Heading his way were the shiny black and white bulky forms of the killer whales. Saoirse froze when he heard the fast clicking noises. Foam and spray hissed.

There was a piercing cry of gulls which startled Seafra awake. She shook some sand from her face and looked around for Saoirse. He was nowhere to be seen. Perhaps he was already in the water. She looked over at the leathery turtle whose neck strained as he stared out to sea.

She sensed the look of terror on his face. Looking to where he was gazing, to her horror she saw the long black dorsal fins tear through the surface. There was no way Saoirse could escape for they had made a circle around him and they were slowly moving in for the kill.

Saoirse spun around to see if he could find a gap. There was no way out of the deadly trap. The orcas slowed to a stop, like a pack of wolves planning their next move. All that could be seen above the surface were the fins, some taller and straighter than others, waiting to attack.

Seafra howled in despair as the one with the tallest fin moved in on Saoirse.

Chapter 12

With a twitch Grypus awoke. He rose on his forepaws and shook his heavy bulk.

For some unknown reason he felt very tense. He'd had a very disturbed sleep, and the most frightful nightmare about demonic creatures with blood-red eyes trying to catch him. He put it down to the octopus he'd eaten before he retired, and reminded himself he must never eat octopus or squid just before bedtime. He took a deep breath, burped and coughed, had a good scratch, then relieved himself. His gurgling stomach signalled to him that he should get some breakfast.

Suddenly his whiskers began to bristle. Something must be up; he always knew when his whiskers bristled that something was not quite right.

A cormorant lifted from the water, flying wave-high along the surface. Grypus twisted his thick neck to see what might have disturbed the bird. Far out to sea the water rippled. Was it a large shoal passing by, he wondered. Heads began to pop up above the wavelets. Grypus could not believe his eyes. Out beyond a sea stack, he could see hundreds of grey seals heading to shore.

'What is going on?' he muttered to himself. Soon they were all around the front of the island, bobbing up and down; nursing mothers, young seals, bulls, cows, different clans and colonies. 'Stop!' Grypus bellowed. 'What is the meaning of this intrusion? Do you not know who I am and that this island belongs to me?' His voice became louder. 'I am . . . '

'We know who you are . . . Lord Grypus, the King of the Seals.'

Grypus was taken aback by the gentle voice of the young mother. Then he recovered. 'Well,' he continued . . . 'if you know who I am you will respect my privacy.'

'We desperately need your help,' another called. 'Only you can give us sanctuary.'

'You are renowned for your strength and power,' said a young bull.

'And your wisdom,' added the young mother who had first spoken to him.

'Can we go on the land?' asked a young pup. 'I'm cold and hungry.'

'It's impossible,' Grypus blurted out. 'The island is mine, and the waters around here couldn't possibly support you lot. You will all just have to return to your own homes.'

'But we cannot go back,' the young mother said sadly. 'We'll all die.'

Grypus demanded to know why they couldn't go back home. Was it on account of the nusham that they made this mass exodus, or was it the orcas who had been seen recently patrolling the seas?

'It's those black devils,' shouted an old cow.

'What black devils?'

'You haven't heard?' said an elder.

'Would I ask if I'd heard?' Grypus snapped. He was usually one of the first to know about any important news from the seas, whether it was a nusham ship sinking, or an oil spill, or some other bad news story. Some of the young seal puppies began to whine and whimper.

'Listen everyone,' said Grypus with authority. 'You can all come ashore and rest up while we try to solve this problem of those black devils.' There were loud cheers and barking; the seals slapped the water in appreciation.

'We knew King Grypus wouldn't let us down,' they shouted in unison.

Grypus beamed back proudly. He was also a little embarrassed by all the adulation.

'Thank you,' the young mother said softly, as she helped to haul her young pup out of the water.

Grypus immediately summoned the elders and anyone else who had seen these black devils. Most of the clans had horror stories to relate of being attacked by the black seals while out catching fish for their families. They had even sent out their strongest, finest young bulls to defend the colonies and rookeries. They never came back. Grypus swallowed hard as they related the events. Mothers, sisters, grandparents, pups - none were spared by these vicious killers.

One seal named Zolak, known for his wisdom, believed it was some terrible nusham experiment using seals that went horribly wrong.

'I knew the nusham would be behind this in some way,' Grypus flared. 'But why,' he asked, 'did the seals want to prey on their own kind?'

Again Zolak had a theory. The black seals believed that they were lacking something in their immune system and that the only way they could prolong their lives was to feed on other seals.

'Disgusting,' said Grypus.

'I also believe their brain may have been affected,' Zolak added. 'And that's why they are such cold-blooded killers.'

'Yes, I think you might be right there,' said Grypus. 'That's the conclusion I would have arrived at also.' Looking around, the island was alive with a mass of movement. Seals had occupied nearly every inch. Grypus looked at the nursing mothers, the old seals, the young cows and bulls, and the rest. Their faces were tense. There was fear in their eyes. None of the younger ones wanted to play about in the surf. It was a sorry state indeed. But what could he do to help them?

He posted sentries at strategic points of the island to keep a good lookout. He ordered twenty of the strong young seals at a time to follow him out to sea to get some food to feed the large herds. The young seals were reluctant to venture back into the waters. They feared death behind every wave.

Grypus bellowed an order that they line up and follow him, which they did without hesitation. 'I know all the hot spots the shoals like to move about in.'

That evening all the seals were well-fed thanks to Grypus and the other bulls. Soon they settled down to sleep. Grypus lay exhausted; every muscle in his body ached. As he lay panting, his thoughts were for young Saoirse; he hoped he was safe and well.

The young mother pulled herself over to the old seal. 'I would like to thank you again,' she said softly. 'On behalf of us all.'

'It's the least I could do, being the King of the Seals,' he said proudly. She introduced herself as Clionabh. 'Delighted to make your acquaintance,' he said. Suddenly his face contorted as he felt a pain dart up his back.

'Are you all right?' she enquired, genuinely concerned.

'Oh, it's just these old bones. They're not able for all that concentrated fishing. I usually have only myself to fend for. Now my family has suddenly increased overnight,' he smiled.

'There may be more coming,' she said in serious tones. 'When word spreads that Grypus' island is a sanctuary.'

He gave a deep sigh. 'Dear oh dear, I don't know what's to be done.'

'Just try to relax,' she said warmly. 'And I'll ease out those stiff joints.' She began to run her foreflipper gently up and down his spine, then nosed along his shoulders.

Grypus began to feel immediate relief. 'Ah, that's marvellous,' he said. Soon he drifted into a deep, relaxed sleep, snoring loudly.

Chapter 13

'You were born under a lucky star,' said Lutra. 'No question about it. What happened yesterday will go down in folklore.'

Saoirse laughed loudly. 'It's just that you and Grypus taught me how to talk my way out of tricky situations.'

'I can't believe it,' said Seafra, licking his face and snuggling up to him. 'Tell us again what exactly happened.'

'Well,' said Saoirse. 'I was in the water like I am now, just about to go fishing for breakfast. I was in no hurry because I knew the two of you were asleep. I was having beautiful thoughts.'

'About what?' Seafra asked.

Saoirse looked a little embarrassed. 'Well . . . ' he said, clearing his throat. ' . . . about us.' Seafra laughed in a teasing fashion. 'My mind was on us . . . ' he continued, ' . . . when suddenly I saw the black fins of the orcas breaking the water.'

'You must have been so frightened,' she offered.

'Well, I was, kind of . . . '

'Kind of?' she repeated in disbelief.

'Well, I guess I was frightened. Terrified to be precise,' he added with a smile. 'Then the biggest of the orcas called the others, who at this stage had made a small circle around me, to a halt. He swam slowly up to me. He was enormous, like a boat. I could feel his breath on my face, and his moist black eyes bore into me. Then he said very quietly. "You are Saoirse, are you not?"'

'He knew your name?' gasped Seafra. 'How amazing!'

'I don't know how, but I stammered out a "yes". He said he

had watched me carrying you,' he nodded at Lutra, 'all the way to the island. "It was a very brave and kind thing you did." His voice seemed more gentle and then he told me he had heard about my plight from Cape, the Sei whale.'

'And I thought killer whales and baleen whales were enemies,' Seafra remarked.

'Some maybe, but these are friends from way back,' Saoirse added.

'Just like me and Cape,' said Lutra.

'You need have no fear of us,' said Saoirse, relating the orca's words.

'That's truly incredible,' said Seafra.

'Well, it proves that the fates look down approvingly on kind acts,' said Lutra. 'There is a natural justice out there.'

'What about the rest of us?' said Seafra. 'You're going to be safe, but the rest of us could end up as breakfast for these powerful cetaceans,' she said in mocking tones.

'No,' said Saoirse, taking her seriously. 'They're leaving soon for the ice kingdom, they said so.'

Then realising by her expression that she was only teasing he added, 'They'd only get indigestion eating someone as cheeky as you.'

Seafra leaped on him, ducking him below the surface. He popped up on the other side of Lutra, snorted and blew out the unwelcome salt water. She laughed loudly.

* * *

As they made their way to Grypus' island they were startled by what they saw. As the island came into view, instead of a quiet isolated island with one old seal resting up they could see a teeming mass of movement. Grey and common seals occupied every inch of the island. What did this mean? Lutra wondered.

As they moved closer loud alarm barks could be heard from different corners of the island. Some seals who were in the water close to the island frantically crashed through the water to the safety of the island, almost trampling other seals in their panic.

Seafra, Saoirse and Lutra swam cautiously towards the island, scanning the seals for any sign of Grypus. As they reached the rocky shore they were greeted with loud growls, snorts and barks.

'Clear off,' yelled some colony members. 'Find another island. There is no more room here.'

'What's happening?' Saoirse yelled. 'Where is Grypus?'

'They're spies,' shouted another. 'They're working for the black demons. Beware, don't let them on.'

'No,' said Lutra. 'We're friends.'

'Maybe we should leave,' said Seafra, looking at all the angry bulls ready for a fight.

'I'm not leaving until I find out what's going on, and what's happened to Grypus,' Saoirse snapped.

'Behind you,' said Seafra.

Saoirse quickly spun around and there was Grypus, his mouth full of fish, followed by about twenty other bull seals carrying fish in their mouths. Grypus tried to speak but only a mumble could be heard. He indicated with his head for them to follow him. They moved in behind him, and the seals on the island made an opening so they could haul themselves out.

Grypus dropped the fish in front of him, and pulled himself up, displaying his huge size and bulk. 'Listen, everyone. This is my grand-nephew Saoirse. He has as much right to be on this island as you, more in fact,' he barked. 'I want you to give him the respect that you accord to me. Is that understood?' They all nodded in unison.

'Also, my dear friend, Lutra. He is someone who knew your grandparents when they were puppies. Yes, even their grandparents. He is respected in the seven seas of the world. I expect the same esteem and respect for the leathery turtle as you give to the elders of your clan.'

Grypus looking at Seafra said: 'And who is this pretty young thing?'

'Seafra is my name, from the clan of Raven's Point in County Wexford.'

'I have heard of them,' said Grypus proudly. 'I visited the area when I was no bigger than young Saoirse here. You are very welcome,' he added.

'Thank you,' said Seafra.

'She's my travelling companion,' explained Saoirse.

'Indeed!' said Grypus, amazed.

'What he means,' said Seafra, 'is that he's my travelling companion.'

Grypus chuckled broadly. Then in an aside to Lutra he said. 'I'm glad I'm not their age again. I couldn't handle it,' he guffawed, then remarked, 'these youngsters have it handy – in my day I had to fight for my females.

'He has a long way to go yet,' said Lutra, 'before he has the worry of a harem.'

'True!' Grypus twitched.

They all settled down to supper and the fish were passed around. There was not enough for each to have a whole fish, so they had to share among themselves. Fights broke out when some bulls complained that others got a bigger piece of the fish than they did.

Grypus gave a long sigh as he listened to the barking, snorting and growling. 'I don't know how long more we can all take being cooped up on this small island. Even the weather is changing. The storm will be coming and it's going to be very difficult hunting for such large numbers. I'm afraid many may die.'

Saoirse asked why had they all gathered on his island. Grypus explained about the reign of terror brought on by the black seals. Saoirse told how he had seen the results of a black seal attack but fortunately had never seen the seals.

They all agreed something must be done, but no one knew what. All attempts to combat the deadly creatures ended in the deaths of their own kind. Grypus laid his heavy frame down and puffed and sighed.

Lutra decided to cheer him up by telling him how Saoirse had rescued him from his entanglement in a lobster pot rope.

'I thought you would have had the sense by now to avoid such things.'

'Well I was avoiding a discarded net when it happened,' Lutra defended himself in mock annoyance.

'Those nusham,' growled Grypus. 'They dump their rubbish in our homes. Supposing we collected up all their litter and dumped it in their homes on land. How would they feel about that? They wouldn't like it one little bit, but it's okay to put our lives at risk.'

Lutra could see old Grypus getting worked up, so he told him the other amazing story of how the killer whales had spared Saoirse's life. Grypus raised his head, mouth open wide in astonishment as Lutra related the entire incident.

A smile broke across Grypus' face. 'Oh it does me good to have you two here again, and you dear Seafra.' He beamed at

her. 'I don't think anyone could top that story,' said Grypus. 'In all my years I've never heard the likes.'

Seafra looked at Saoirse. There was a twinkle in his eye. 'Tell Grypus your experience,' he gestured to Seafra. 'Lutra hasn't heard it either. She too has a story that might equal mine.'

Seafra described how she was swept off the rocks when she was only a week old. Then she explained how she was reared by a nusham and was safely released back into the seas months later.

'These stories get more fantastic . . . I must have had a very sheltered upbringing,' said Grypus. 'You two pups seem to have lived several lives all in one.'

'And they've only just begun,' Lutra smiled.

Seafra's mood changed as Saoirse related how her family had met their untimely end at the hands of the black seals. Her eyes welled with tears as she was reminded of her loss. She moved away down to the shore. Saoirse felt terrible for mentioning it again and hurried down to comfort her. The two sat silently staring out to sea, watching the night move in.

Chapter 14

Saoirse awoke with a start. The shrieks and wails of seals focused his mind on the realisation that something terrible was happening. All the seals had their necks craned towards the sea. There, floating on the water, were the badly mutilated bodies of a band of over thirty common seals.

Seafra was already in the water, checking whether any of them were alive. Sadly, they were all dead. The sight made Seafra retch. She knew who was responsible, it was painfully obvious. Grypus hurried down to see. Saoirse yelled to Seafra to get out of the water. She looked up and beckoned him down.

'Seafra, Seafra!' he yelled again. 'Get out of the water!'

Grypus gasped in terror for, looking beyond the bloated floating corpses, he could see the hordes of vile black creatures moving in for the kill towards Seafra.

All the seals were now shrieking and barking in warning as they could see the black seals getting closer. Saoirse hurried through the seals, pushing them aside to reach the shoreline. Seafra had managed to outswim the black seals and get to shore and safety. Her heart was pounding in her chest. All the seals huddled together at the highest points on the island.

They could hear the terrible laughter and jeering coming from the black hordes as they bobbed up and down in triumph. Then one black seal broke from the others and moved closer to shore. His hideous appearance brought terror to all the seals who could see him clearly. Then he grimaced and spoke in menacing tones.

'My name is Dread, the Dark One! My army has you surrounded. You have two choices. One is to become my subjects and obey my every command without question. The other is to refuse and starve to death, making this sanctuary your tomb. I will give you until sunrise to make your decision. No compromise!' He turned swiftly and joined with the others. They immediately submerged themselves and could not be seen.

A wave of panic spread through the colonies. The elders pleaded with Grypus to do something. One young seal lost its balance and fell from the boulder plopping into the sea. Suddenly the water appeared to boil as the blacks moved in for the kill. There was a loud wail. The young seal was seen no more.

Grypus paced up and down, rocking his body, trying desperately to come up with some solution. None slept that night except for the very young who were not aware of what was happening.

'Maybe if we agreed to their demands, they would spare us,' said one of the elders.

'Forget it!' said Grypus. 'If we agree, they will simply pick us off like ticks on our fur.'

'How can we wait around and watch our families slowly starve to death?' asked another.

'Perhaps if I distracted them in some way,' said Lutra. 'It would give some of the younger ones a chance to try and sneak up on them, play them at their own game.'

'Impossible,' said another elder. 'They have the strength of demons.'

'No, dear friend,' said Grypus. 'We cannot risk your life.'

'I'm old and have lived a full life,' said Lutra.

'Even if he wants to allow himself to become a sacrifice for us, I cannot see you convincing the young bulls to attack. They already know what the outcome would be!' said another older seal.

'Maybe we should try and sleep on it,' said Seafra. 'Who knows what ideas may come to us during the night.'

'Who can sleep with that worry hanging over us?' another grumbled.

'It's an excellent idea,' said Grypus. 'Why should we allow those vermin to rob us of our sleep. I want everyone to just relax and calm down. Tomorrow we will be able to think more clearly,' he said loudly. 'Now, pass the word along.'

'They won't risk coming on shore, not with all of us,' Saoirse offered.

As the order was spread through the herds they soon began to settle and closed their eyes. Grypus followed suit, and got himself as comfortable as he could, since he was not sleeping by his favourite rock which had been taken over by several pups. Lutra crashed down in exhaustion. Seafra decided she should practise what she preached. There was not much point in her sitting fretting away, so she laid her head down and began to listen to the soothing sounds of the waves. Soon she drifted into sleep.

Heavy black clouds banked high in the sky, blocking out the light of the moon and stars. Saoirse opened one eye. He could hear heaving and snoring, some seals were making fretting sounds, others were tossing and turning in fitful sleep. It was crazy that such a strong proud race of sea creatures should be reduced to this – afraid to venture into their own marine world, denied a basic right to get on with life.

Saoirse had made his own plans, he was not going to wait around and let some vile creatures decide his and his friends' fate. Checking that Seafra, Grypus and Lutra were truly asleep, he eased his way down to the water's edge. He scanned the inky black water for any visible sign of the black seals. He knew they were out there somewhere, but where he did not know. He only hoped that they too might be asleep.

Silently he waded into the dark water. He could hear the sound of his own heart pounding in his chest. He moved with a feeling of dread that any moment he would be pounced upon. His body shook uncontrollably as he moved away from the safety of the island. He could hear the swish of waves hitting the island. One part of him wanted to go back, leave the problem to the others, another part spurred him on.

Saoirse wasn't afraid of death, but he was afraid of failure. His plan seemed more and more crazy as he moved out into the heavy swells. Did he really believe he could pull off such a fantastical idea?

Black menacing eyes watched his progress from beneath the surface. 'One of them is fleeing from the island,' whispered Dread. 'He must not escape.'

Saoirse began to feel more relaxed the further he moved out into the deep. He assumed the black seals were close to the island and that he had slipped through their net. He moved with greater determination, riding the waves, putting a great distance between himself and the island, unaware that he was being followed by the black hordes.

'Hunt him down! I want the taste of his blood in my mouth before dawn,' said Dread, as they blazed through the water.

Saoirse thought he heard the sound of movement, like a large group moving through the water. Panic set in. He looked once over his shoulder only to see a pod of white-sided dolphins cross behind him, moving in steady unison through the black waters. He stopped momentarily to watch as they moved westwards out of sight. Then he propelled himself on, scanning and listening as he travelled through the hollow of the night.

'We've lost him,' said one black seal to Dread.

'He's out there,' said Dread, exploding into a gigantic rage as they surfaced for air.

'We were tracking him but when those dolphins passed we became distracted.'

'He's still near,' growled Dread. 'I can feel him.' His red jaws thirsted for the blood of this seal that dared to challenge him by trying to escape.

'I see him,' cried another.

Dread sniggered slyly. 'See, I told you I could feel him. Now move in on our quarry, and leave me the choicest parts.'

Their voices carried on the wind. Saoirse turned to see the black heads in between the waves. The clouds began to clear and the stars became visible beacons again. Saoirse knew this could be his final hour. The black hordes must have been tracking him all the time. He struggled to move faster. His plan was falling to pieces for there was no sign of the orcas anywhere. He had hoped to convince them to help him destroy the deadly seals. If any creatures could, they could.

But his hopes began to crumble as the black seals closed in. The orcas had said they were leaving for the ice kingdom. He resigned himself to the fact that they must have left the previous day. His only hope now was to try and find somewhere to hide, but where? The nearest place was Grypus' island. But that would mean trying to get past his pursuers without them getting him.

Then to his joy he saw a fishing vessel on the horizon. If he could get to it perhaps he could hide alongside or underneath it. He feared the nusham, but not as much as he feared the black seals. Saoirse figured the black seals would not go anywhere near nusham. It was his only hope.

Propelling his aching form through the water with all the speed he could muster, he headed straight for the boat.

'He's getting away and heading for the nusham boat,' cried one of the black seals.

'Cut him off!' ordered Dread.

Saoirse saw the light of the ship getting closer. He quickly took a glance over his shoulder. The black seals seemed to be slowing down. He gave a deep sigh of relief. With a final burst of effort he could be hiding below the ship in a matter of minutes.

Then to his horror he came face to face with a black seal. Saoirse gaped as the black seal lunged at him, but he twisted his body in time to avoid the deadly fangs that missed his soft fur by inches. He heard the sounds of savage roars from behind him. With blinding speed the black seals were upon him.

Their leader gave out a demonic roar and struck Saoirse savagely in the back. An arrow of pain shot through the young seal as another black seal struck a savage blow to the back of his neck. With his hind flipper Saoirse kicked out at one of his assailants, winding one with a well-placed kick to the stomach. It shot to the surface gasping and coughing.

Two black seals gripped Saoirse by his foreflippers. He struggled to free himself but they were too strong for him. He tried to bite at them but they succeeded in avoiding his attacks. Dread moved slowly over to Saoirse, and ran his foreflipper down his chest, piercing his fur with his sharp nails.

Saoirse tried to stifle the desire to scream although the pain was unbearable as the nails tore deeply into his skin. His face contorted at the agonising sensation of another cruel bite from behind. So powerful was the impact that Saoirse momentarily lost consciousness. As he came around, the nightmarish face of Dread loomed over him.

'Gasp your last breath, fool. Or should I say hero!' The other seals sniggered. 'You are about to become my supper.' His hellish jaws parted as his eyes gleamed with an evil thrill.

'I pity you,' said Saoirse. 'You have nothing to offer life only destruction. Do your worst.'

'Never fear,' said Dread, 'I intend to.'

Saoirse closed his eyes knowing the end was near.

There was no time to call out a warning cry. The astonished black hordes watched in terror as a pack of orcas raced through the waters. Dread was arrested from his murderous intent by the shrieks and squeals of the black seals being tossed and torn to shreds.

'Escape!' he cried, as they tried to get away from their deadly enemies.

The orcas swept across the water like a raging storm. There were loud sounds of rolling and thrashing as the moving orcas came upon the black seals. The water churned into a welter of foam as the ferocious battle continued. Jaws snapped and flesh ripped. One by one the black seals were dispatched until there was only one left, Dread, their leader. He had dived several fathoms in search of a shipwreck so he could escape from the killer whales.

His departure did not go unnoticed. The leader of the orcas dived in hot pursuit, after the last of the vile creatures. There was no way the orca was going to let this rogue escape.

Dread had succeeded in locating a large wreck where he could hide, scattering several conger eels as he pushed through a gaping hole in the hull. His red eyes scanned the dark water for any sign of the killer whales. Visibility was poor, but he felt secure. There were so many of his army the whales would never notice one slip away amid all that confusion.

There was a strong smell of blood in the water. Dread realised all his kind must have been destroyed. Still, he could easily bully other seals into submission and soon he would have a strong army again to wage war on whoever he fancied.

Like a black apparition the orca appeared beside the wreck. Dread reeled in horror as the whale crashed through the rotten wood, seizing him by the head. The orca shook the body violently, then snapped it in two like a twig with his powerful jaws.

Moving back to the surface where the other orcas lay about silently, he spied the young seal floating silently on the surface. Circling slowly he could see blood oozing from Saoirse's gaping wounds. The orcas watched as their leader gently hoisted the young seal's body onto his domed head.

Chapter 15

Seafra awoke still bleary-eyed, having spent most of the night tossing and turning. South-east winds had freshened since early light. Seafra raised her head high to feel the breeze rush over her face.

Looking around she could see that most of the seals were awake, huddled together for comfort and support, some stretching and grooming, the young pups suckling their mothers.

Alongside her Lutra and Grypus were still dozing, but Saoirse was gone. Perhaps he was out swimming. She raised her body to try and see above the teeming mass of seals, then panic set in as she remembered the black seals. Scanning the choppy water; she could see no sign of Saoirse or any black seals.

Suddenly one of the elder seals came thrashing through the groups. 'Grypus! Grypus!' he bellowed.

Grypus raised his head and opened his eyes slowly. 'What's up?' he snorted, annoyed at being so abruptly awakened.

'Your grand-nephew Saoirse . . . '

'Yes, what is it?' Grypus demanded, seeing the stress of the elder's face.

'He . . . '

'What?' said Grypus. 'Tell me now.'

'He's gone . . . '

'Gone where?'

'Gone over to the other side,' said the elder.

'What the devil do you mean?' Grypus growled.

'A young bull saw him slip into the water during the

midnight hour . . . and the black seals left with him.'

'It's a lie,' said Seafra, showing her anger. 'If Saoirse left, it was to draw the black seals away from the island.'

Lutra was now awake and listening to every word being said. He piped up. 'Saoirse is the bravest, kindest young seal I've ever encountered in my long life.'

'See!' said Grypus, puffing and snorting.

'Well, it's only natural they would defend your grand-nephew,' a young bull retorted. 'But the fact is, and I have it from a reliable source, that Saoirse has gone with the black seals.'

'How dare you say such things about any of my clan, especially Saoirse. Withdraw that remark or I'll challenge you to a fight right now.'

'He's a traitor,' the bull shouted.

Then another yelled out: 'Saoirse is a traitor to us all.'

'Traitor! Traitor! Traitor!' the herd screamed loudly.

Grypus swivelled his head. 'I'll challenge anyone who calls my grand-nephew a traitor,' he roared as deeply as he possibly could.

Seafra had pulled herself up into a threatening stance. Lutra made chomping noises trying to sound tough.

Another elder said quietly to Grypus. 'You cannot take us all on.'

'We'll go down trying,' said Grypus defiantly.

'Can I ask you just one question?' said another elder member in a calm tone. 'How come if Saoirse didn't join the black seals we did not hear fighting and roaring during the night?'

'Perhaps Saoirse somehow slipped through their defences.'

'Ten of our strongest were destroyed like little pups when they challenged them, and you are saying one young seal could manage it!'

Grypus snorted. 'You forget he has my blood in him.'

Then another young bull challenged Grypus by asking what was Saoirse doing, slipping away during the night?

Grypus could not answer but said in defence he must have had a very good reason, that's all.

'If it wasn't to join the black seals, then perhaps it was to save his own skin! Not giving a limpet for the safety of his lady love here, or all the other seals?'

'You keep talking like that,' said Seafra, 'and you will have to answer to me.'

The large bull sniggered. 'Fiery young cow, aren't we?'

'Look!' a mother seal shrieked.

All eyes turned to the sea. There was wails, hisses and snorts as they spied the killer whales heading towards the island. They watched them cutting through the distant waves with tremendous acceleration. Soon they would be upon them, circling the island.

One of the elders shouted out in panic. 'We are all doomed. The killer whales are coming to join the black seals. We're all going to die.'

All the seals began to panic, shrieking and howling in terror at the sight of the powerful hunters.

'We're all like sitting ducks,' yelled another bull. 'We won't be able to hunt! We'll starve!'

'Silence!' Grypus bellowed.

It looked as if the orcas were about to bank onto the island. The seals recoiled in terror as they pushed and crushed to the back of the island.

The leader of the killer whales raised his colossal bulk out of the water. To her horror Seafra could see the broken form of Saoirse where he now lay by the base of the whale's dorsal fin.

There was a deadly silence except for the wind churning up the water. 'I have returned your young seal, Saoirse,' the leader said solemnly. 'He came for our help to rid the seas of the black seals. Regrettably we were too late to save Saoirse. Sadly this young fella is mortally wounded and I fear he is not going to make it through the day.' The orca slipped his mighty frame backwards, allowing the disturbed water to wash over Saoirse and easing him to shore.

Saoirse's twisted form lay like dead seaweed on the shore. Seafra hurried to him and gently nosed him, then licked his face tenderly. Tears filled her eyes at the sight of the savage bites inflicted on his beautiful body.

The leader pulled himself into an upright position in the water, then said, 'Today we leave for the ice kingdom. You need not fear the black hordes for they are all destroyed.' The seals could not believe their ears. Their deadly enemies were no more. 'We'll take our leave,' said the orca. 'You can be proud of your young hero; he is a credit to his race. His name will be imprinted on the wind, waves and rocks.'

'Thank you,' said Grypus. He began to sob. Seafra snuggled up to him and they both wept.

The seals cheered and slapped their flippers in gratitude as the orcas silently sailed away. They waved their flukes in friendship then disappeared into the deep. An eerie silence descended on the island as one by one the seals filed past to pay their respects to Saoirse. Some of the elders who had accused Saoirse of being a traitor apologised sincerely. Grypus accepted their apologies on behalf of his grand-nephew.

Lutra made a pillow of sand for Saoirse and gently eased his head on to it.

Seafra nudged and licked at Saoirse's wounds, then gave out

a loud howl at the elements. 'Why?' she pleaded to Grypus. 'It's not fair. He had so much to offer to life.' Grypus rubbed his flipper across her back trying to comfort her. 'What can we do?' she pleaded, staring with tear-filled eyes.

'Nothing my child, but weep. And be grateful for his wonderful life, however brief.'

* * *

There was a great sense of relief among the seals. The young were back playing and frolicking in the water, sure in the knowledge that the terrible danger of the black seals was gone. Mothers could rest easily knowing their young were safe. Young bulls began to display and make shows of strength to impress the young cows. The older ones talked and debated all morning about how the black seals must have come about and more importantly, their own sense of joy at the idea of returning home and living a normal life again.

The elders called for a council meeting in the afternoon. Grypus, Seafra and Lutra were invited to attend. Seafra declined; she was keeping a lonely vigil with the dying form of her beloved.

In the early afternoon, the elders met and formed a circle with Grypus and Lutra in the centre, the position of honour. One of the elders opened the meeting. 'Welcome brothers, sisters, dear friends. I don't have to remind you all of the fears, terror and anxiety of recent events we've suffered. The heavens know we've experienced strange events in the past . . . '

'But nothing like the sheer terror of the black hordes . . . ' another elder interjected.

'We'll be brief and to the point. Grypus, we are all eternally grateful to you for allowing us the safety your island offered. You are truly the King of the Seals. You fed us and kept our fears at bay. We are deeply grateful. We have decided to leave at first light and return home.'

Another added: 'I'm sure you will be delighted to have the peace and quiet of the island to yourself again.'

'Well, I cannot deny that,' Grypus retorted cheerfully.

Then another spoke. 'We are all deeply saddened by what has happened to your only grand-nephew. He was a true hero. He will be remembered with great fondness. Now, I think if there is no other business we'll take our leave for the present, and perhaps you would join us for supper in your honour before we depart.'

'Before everyone leaves,' said Lutra clearing his throat. 'Could I ask you all to assist in a special ceremony for our dear Saoirse?'

'Of course,' said one of the elders. 'We will be honoured to take part in the ritual for the dead.'

Lutra gave a faint smile. 'That's not exactly what I had in mind.'

'What did you have in mind, dear friend?' Grypus enquired.

The elders listened intently as the old turtle related how he once visited a far away island near the ice kingdom where a young beluga whale lay dying from a harpoon wound. The old sage there suggested to the other whales there that they should hold her in their thoughts and at night take her into their dream world. There they should ask the ancient ones to heal her. Well, they all did as the sage suggested. Hundreds of them took the young princess beluga into their dreams. Next morning just at sunrise, like a miracle she was healed.

'Well, I've never heard anything so preposterous in all my life,' one elder guffawed.

'It sounds like black magic to me,' said another nervously.

'Only good comes out of good,' said Lutra, disappointed at their response. He turned and crawled away down to the shore.

'Listen,' said Grypus. 'It sounds fantastical to me as well, but I'm prepared to try anything to save my grand-nephew. I'd willingly give up my own life.' He followed after Lutra.

'They're grasping at straws,' sighed another elder.

'Maybe we should try it for the sake of Grypus,' an old female suggested.

'It wouldn't hurt to dream,' said another. 'It's the least we could do.'

Seafra's head lay across the crinkled body of Saoirse. She could still hear the faint heartbeat, but he had lost all consciousness. She hoped he was not in pain. It would be a happy release for him to pass over, instead of this slow lingering death, she thought. Yet her heart did not want him to go quietly into the arms of death. She wanted him to fight. She scolded herself for being so selfish. She had refused supper and waited by her love instead. The night crept in across the sky.

Suddenly she became aware of eyes staring at her. Looking around she could see hundreds and hundreds of seals all gathered around, staring at her. They stood in solemn silence. Seafra was baffled as to why they were doing this. Had they not already paid their last respects to her lover?

Lutra eased his way over to her. 'Don't be alarmed, Seafra, but the night is approaching and I've asked all the colonies, rookeries and clans to take part in a special ceremony before they leave in the morning.'

'He still clings to life,' said Seafra sadly. 'Can the ceremony of the dead not wait until he departs from these shores?' A tear escaped from her eye.

'Please trust me,' said Lutra, unable to hold back his own tears.

'Because I know you love him dearly . . . ' said Seafra, 'I will gladly follow your wishes.'

'Thank you for that,' said Lutra tenderly.

Under the stars the seals stood silent as stones. Grypus nodded to Lutra to say a few words.

'I thank you all for agreeing to take part in this ceremony. I would ask you to close your eyes and journey into the inner chambers of your mind, at the same time holding our dear Saoirse in your heart. Think him well, wish him well, ask the source of all life to heal his broken form. Don't see his wounds, but see him whole and well. That is all I have to say except to urge you to lay aside doubt, scepticism and anxiety. Give

yourself over to faith. Become one in thought and action.'
Under the shadow of darkness they became united in one
purpose, to hold the young seal in their vision.

Seafra looked at Grypus and Lutra who had closed their eyes
and were breathing deeply. A cloak of peace spread over the
island. Even the noises from the waves seemed to cease. They
plunged themselves into a deep silence most had never
experienced before.

Saoirse's spirit journeyed to the edge of the abyss. The waters
below were black, then he saw movement. The black seals
wriggled and squirmed like reptiles. Their red eyes glowed and
the jaws gaped to show their sharp jagged teeth. They leaped
up to snatch him down. He tried to pull away but was unable
to move. Clouds rumbled making strange, vile shapes, talons
reached out to tear at him. Screams pierced through his mind.
Lightning tore the sky. Waves of gloom lifted him up, hurtling
him into a blood-red landscape. He was being tossed on the
ocean of death. He tried to swim but his body would not
respond. He saw death standing like a giant black seal whose
head was a skull, the sockets empty.

'Death will be swift and brutal,' he heard a voice sounding in
his head. He felt himself drawn towards the skull. It grew
bigger and bigger as he moved nearer. The sockets were now
tunnels of black which he was being drawn into. He tried to
pull away. The power was too strong, pulling him in. The black
seals were there, inside the tunnels, waiting and lurking around
the edges of darkness.

He screamed. His lungs hurt. He was being thrust deeper.
How could he free himself from this alien world of blackness
and despair? Then he heard voices calling, faintly at first then
getting louder. Sweet, beautiful warm voices, like gentle spring

rainfall on a calm sea.

He recognised the voice of his lovely companion, Seafra. Grypus could be heard too. Yes, and Lutra. How comforting they were. He would not be afraid any more if he could hold the sound of their voices in his head; he could endure hell itself.

Then there was a sudden explosion of light that flooded the tunnels, washing him back through the empty sockets. The sky was a rainbow of colour spilling down like a giant waterfall. Below the sea was a golden light. The waves made beautiful, enchanting music. Shafts of light shot through him.

He felt a great ecstasy. He was being carried by the light to a new tunnel. Death sat there, not a fearful creature but a gentle being, a friend that smiled warmly, showing him a world of exquisite beauty. His family could be seen swimming in the beautiful waters that gently ebbed and flowed to a mysterious shore. Then his parents swam towards him and greeted him, showering him with love and warmth. 'We are so proud of you,' Mara said, hugging him lightly. His father beamed brightly at him. 'Is it my time?' he asked softly. 'I'm not afraid!' His parents smiled back. 'Not yet. Your earthly life has not run its course, my darling.' Saoirse remained motionless as the images began to fade from his sight.

Saoirse suddenly began to fall at great speed from his celestial plane. He did not know where, nor could he prevent it happening. Images hurtled past the corner of his eyes, too fast for him to comprehend. Panic set in as he seemed to accelerate through strange worlds. He wanted to scream but could not find his voice.

Then in an instant everything had stopped. He knew he was lying somewhere, but he had no idea where. He could sense light beyond his eyelids and the murmur of gentle voices. He felt a gentle breeze across his face that made him shiver. Slowly he opened his eyelids. To his great joy he saw the beautiful face of Seafra peering down at him. Tears ran from her face and splashed onto his eye.

'Is this another vision?' he asked softly.

'No, dear Saoirse. It's all very real. You've come back to us.' She gently nuzzled him.

There was an explosion of noise as the seals cheered and clapped at the sight of Saoirse trying to raise himself from the ground.

'Steady, dear boy,' said Grypus. 'You've been through the mill.' Lutra gave a sigh of relief. Grypus patted him hard on the carapace. 'Well done, dear Lutra. I don't know how you did it, but you did it.'

'I did nothing,' said the old turtle. 'Only made a suggestion.' Seafra licked Lutra and Grypus warmly.

'It's a miracle,' said a young mother to another. 'All his wounds have completely vanished.'

'The power of thought,' said one of the elders.

'The power of auto-suggestion,' said another.

'The power of placing your trust in the fates,' said an old grandmother.

'What happened?' Saoirse enquired.

'Oh nothing much,' said Seafra. 'You were sleeping, as usual,' she said in mocking tones.

'I've had the strangest dreams, some horrible, others beautiful.'

'We have a lot to talk about,' said Grypus.

'Could it wait until after breakfast?' Saoirse wondered, then added, 'I'm ravenous!'

They all broke into uncontrollable laughter.

Chapter 16

The sun climbed above the horizon and flooded the island with its golden light. Gulls called noisily from the sky having flown from their night perches. Shaking the sleep from their wings they went in search of food. Grypus stirred, yawned and stretched. In the wave tops just beyond the island he noticed two heads bob up and down in the dazzling light. It was Saoirse and Seafra clowning about. It filled his tired eyes with happiness to see them so contented and happy again.

'The joy of youth,' said Lutra who moved up beside him.

'It's truly amazing how these young folk bounce back after all that has happened.'

'Too true,' said Lutra.

Saoirse and Seafra had been out earlier for some quiet fishing. Grypus was delighted to see his breakfast waiting for him just at the shoreline. Several flounders lay there and some jellyfish for Lutra. All the seals had returned to their coves, inlets and islands. Grypus was delighted to have the place to himself again, he didn't mind admitting.

After breakfast Saoirse offered to show Seafra the island where he was born. He hadn't returned there since the nusham massacred his clan. Seafra had asked him several times about the place, so he decided to overcome his anxieties and make a return visit. The weather was mild and the seas calm, so they decided to make the journey after breakfast.

Before they left, Grypus told them that they were to consider this island their home, and no matter wherever they roamed to remember this. If they wanted to have a family, here is where they could bring them up in safety.

'Let's not rush things,' said Seafra jokingly. 'I might not be able to put up with him over the coming years.'

'Oh I don't mean now,' said Grypus awkwardly. 'I mean in the distant future when you are fully grown . . . '

'I know what you mean, dear Grypus.' She nuzzled him affectionately.

'We'll be back by nightfall,' said Saoirse. 'Don't think you're going to get rid of us that easily.'

Seafra nuzzled Lutra. 'Thank you again,' she said softly, 'for bringing him back to me.'

As they approached the island Saoirse began to tremble as the memories came flooding back. Seafra sensed this and nibbled gently along his body, licking his face. 'It's all right, we're together, come what may.'

Saoirse nuzzled her. Then, scanning the island, he could not believe his eyes. Several seals stared back at them.

'Look!' said Seafra, as a baby seal nuzzled closer to her mother's flanks.

A big bull seal suddenly popped up in front of them. They were both startled. The old bull could see that this very young bull was no threat to him or his harem, but he remained very alert and almost threatening. 'What is your business here?' he demanded to know.

'We just came to visit,' said Saoirse. 'I was born on this island.'

'Really,' said the old bull, a little less defensive now. 'Well, when we arrived the island was deserted. It is an ideal place for my wives to have their young and raise them in safety.'

'Yes, indeed,' said Saoirse.

'So you were born here,' the old bull mused, then added, 'You are welcome to feast with us.'

Seafra and Saoirse followed the big bull on to the island. The place seemed so strange to Saoirse now. Tides and winds had obliterated any signs of his clan. The old bull introduced them to his ten wives and their pups. Saoirse was glad to see life had returned to the island. It's what his family would have wanted as well. The old bull explained that they had only recently arrived and it was like a miracle to find a beautiful island like this deserted.

'It was a gift from the great spirit,' said one of the wives. They explained how they'd had to leave their home because of a terrible oil-spill from one of those nusham tankers. Many of their kind had died and they'd thought they were all doomed until they reached these waters and found this island.

'We are so happy for you,' said Saoirse.

'Where do you live?' enquired one of the mothers.

'Not too far away,' said Seafra. 'On an island called Grypus island.'

'So we're neighbours,' said the bull cheerfully.

'You could say that,' smiled Saoirse.

After they had shared food together Seafra asked if they'd heard of the black seals. 'We haven't,' was the reply. 'But not having been here long, hopefully we will meet them some time,' the bull offered,

Seafra and Saoirse laughed. The other seals looked puzzled. Saoirse and Seafra explained what had happened in recent times to the astonishment of those listening.

'And we thought that the oil-spill was the worst thing that could happen to us,' said a mother in anxious tones.

'Well, rest assured,' said Seafra. 'The black seals are well and truly gone.'

By late afternoon it was time for them to leave. They thanked the seals for their hospitality and promised to visit them again soon.

'You're always welcome back here,' said the bull to Saoirse and Seafra as they slipped back into the sea.

As they moved away from the island Saoirse was left with feelings of joy and loss. Joy that the island was alive again with the sounds of seal pups wailing for food. Loss that not a hint remained of his clan. They moved silently through the water. Then Seafra suggested they visit the great island before returning home. She began to mimic the bull saying how he would like to meet the black seals. Saoirse and herself broke into uncontrollable laughter as they made their way towards the mainland.

They passed the silent cliffs that earlier in the year buzzed with the sounds of seabirds nesting. A lone hooded crow could be seen walking the shingle beach in search of storm casualties or discarded scraps. They could see the homes of the nusham dotted along the coast. Smoke curled from some of the bungalows, smudging the sky.

Seafra and Saoirse explored an inlet where upturned dinghies lay about on the sandy shore.

'Too many signs of nusham for my liking,' said Saoirse. 'I think we'll leave.'

High up a ladder Michael Keane was replacing tiles on the roof of their bungalow; they had been blown off during the recent storm. His wife, Bridie, came out with a mug of tea and some scones.

'There's Daddy,' she said, pointing up to him. The baby pulled at her mother's hair.

'Aoife, Aoife,' Michael called from the roof. The baby smiled back.

'I'll leave the tea here,' said Bridie. 'Don't forget your parents are coming for dinner.'

'I'm nearly done,' said Michael. As he climbed down the ladder he noticed the two seals out beyond the rocks. 'Seals!'

He hurried into the house, passing his wife who had just returned to the kitchen. Picking up his rifle from his workshop, he then pulled out drawers looking for bullets.

'What is it?' his wife enquired, becoming alarmed.

'Seals, that's what.' Michael began to load the rifle and move outdoors. Bridie hurried out after him. She could see the two seals playing about in the seaweed. He raised the gun and took aim.

'Leave them!' she pleaded, placing her hand across the barrel of the rifle and lowering it. He glared at the seals, then looked at his wife and baby daughter, who was stretching out her arms indicating she wanted to be held by him.

A broad grin broke across his face. 'You're right,' he sighed. 'I suppose they have as much right to be here as any of us.'

His wife kissed him and took the rifle. Michael held their baby, then pointing out to sea he said, 'Look, Aoife! Seals!'

———— * ————

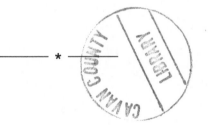

THE SEA TRILOGY

Look out for other books in THE SEA TRILOGY

• *The Mermaid's Song*   • *When the Sea Calls*